W9-ABV-777

A Comedy of Clerical Errors

Fred Secombe was born in Swansea in 1918 and ordained in 1942. The vicar of various parishes and a Prebendary of St Paul's Cathedral, he was also the founder of three Gilbert & Sullivan Companies and won the Waterford International Festival of Light Opera Award for Utopia Ltd in 1968. He now lives in Cardiff.

Also by Fred Secombe

HOW GREEN WAS MY CURATE
A CURATE FOR ALL SEASONS
GOODBYE CURATE
HELLO, VICAR!

A Comedy of
Clerical Errors

FRED SECOMBE

Illustrated by Maxine Rogers

Fount
An Imprint of HarperCollins*Publishers*

To the vanished valleys species –
the South Wales miner

Fount Paperbacks is an Imprint of
HarperCollins*Religious*
Part of HarperCollins*Publishers*
77–85 Fulham Palace Road,
Hammersmith, London W6 8JB

First edition published in Great Britain in 1994
by Michael Joseph Ltd.

This edition first published in Great Britain
in 1995 by Fount Paperbacks
3 5 7 9 8 6 4 2

A catalogue record for this book is
available from the British Library

ISBN 0 00 627876 0

Printed in Great Britain by
HarperCollinsManufacturing Glasgow

'May the blessing of God Almighty, the Father, the Son and the Holy Ghost be upon you and remain with you from this day forth and for evermore,' intoned the parson in a quavery voice. The dewdrop on his red nose glinted in the morning sunshine. It had been there throughout the marriage service. Its owner was loath to part with it either by the use of a handkerchief or even a sniff. The embarrassed bridegroom had tried to draw the officiant's attention to it by sign language during the opening hymn, only to be met with an uncomprehending stare. What compounded the embarrassment was the fact that the dewdrop belonged to his father and furthermore that the best man was his vicar.

Charles Wentworth-Baxter was my curate and apparently friendless since he had asked me to be his best man for the ceremony which was taking place in my own church. His father, Canon Septimus Wentworth-Baxter, recently retired, had come down from Yorkshire to preside at the nuptials of his son and his bride, Nurse Bronwen Williams, a newly qualified SRN. After the blessing the canon plus his dewdrop proceeded into the vestry, to be followed by the wedding party. The bridal retinue was in keeping with the bride's profession, consisting of Eleanor, my wife, the local doctor, and matron of honour for the occasion, together with the two bridesmaids, also newly qualified SRNs. Mr and Mrs Amos Williams, proud parents of the bride, brought up the rear.

The bridegroom, who wore a clerical dress-suit borrowed from his father and two sizes too large for him, spent the first few minutes in the vestry in a passionate embrace with his beloved while the rest of us talked among ourselves. It was a cough from the canon which ended the love scene.

'Back to earth, Charles,' he commanded, and produced a large handkerchief from his pocket to remove the dewdrop with a trumpeting blow. This relaxed the bride who then had to endure six more embraces of much shorter duration while her husband was signing the register.

'Beautiful wedding!' said Mrs Olive Williams to my wife. 'Our Bronwen looks lovely, doesn't she? My sister-in-law made the dress (she's a tailoress, you see). Cost us most of our coupons, I can tell you – but it's worth it, isn't it?'

It was Easter Monday, 1948 and clothing coupons were not in plentiful supply.

Before my wife could reply, the bride's mother carried on with her monologue. 'Mind, I'd always hoped she would have been married in Tabernacle with the Reverend Josiah Jones-Evans doing the service. Strict Baptist we are, as you know. Still, the Reverend Jones-Evans is down here for the wedding and we've asked him to say a few words at the reception. It's very kind of your husband to let us have the church hall for the meal. We wouldn't dream of going to a hotel for it where they serve strong drink, and fancy Charles's friends with that Gilbert Society offering to serve at the tables and put everything ready beforehand. They've been a great help, I must say, and didn't they sing that sacred song nicely at the end?'

There was a look of desperation on Eleanor's face

2

which prompted Bronwen to intervene. 'Mam, would you like to hold my bouquet while I sign the register?' As Mrs Williams went to the bride to collect the bouquet, my wife moved swiftly to join the two bridesmaids who were in animated conversation in one corner of the vestry.

'Shall we have the bride now, please? Or may I say, my daughter-in-law?' The canon motioned Bronwen to the desk on which reposed the marriage register. Before she sat in the chair which the bridegroom had vacated, the old clergyman embraced her warmly. He turned to his son and said, 'I hope you realize, Charles, that you are a very lucky young man.' Bronwen blushed and took her seat. Charles was buttonholed by his mother-in-law.

I remained firmly anchored with Amos Williams who was proving to be a surprisingly rounded person for a 'Strict Baptist'. He was very knowledgeable about Welsh male-voice choirs and even about radio programmes like *Itma*, displaying a keen sense of humour. Evidently the fervour for the Baptist cause was confined to Mrs Williams. At one time it had infected her daughter who decided to become a medical missionary only to be turned down by the Society for lack of qualifications. Instead she was persuaded by Charles that she could serve God just as well in Pontywen, as a curate's wife. They were going to live in the curate's house largely furnished with furniture provided by the bridegroom's father, a widower who had retired from his large old vicarage to live in a cottage in the Yorkshire countryside.

With the ceremonial details duly recorded, the procession formed up to leave the vestry. Since Charles was motherless, I suggested that Mr and Mrs Williams should form one couple, Eleanor and I the next, with the two bridesmaids following the bride and groom. Canon Wentworth-Baxter had said that he would rather not join the parade but would leave by the back door of the vestry and meet us outside the church for the photographs. The signal was given to Mr Greenfield the organist who launched into an inaccurate rendering of Mendelssohn's *Wedding March*. Through its discordances my wife murmured to me that she intended to avoid Mrs Williams for the rest of the proceedings if she could.

Outside the church, Humphries the Snap, the local photographer, was waiting to 'record the happy event for future posterity', to use his favourite phrase, repeated at every wedding he attended. He was wearing his long grey overcoat despite the warm sunshine. The coat was as ancient and as indispensable as his big box camera, resting on a tripod together with its voluminous cloth under which he would disappear like a stage magician.

A large crowd of spectators had gathered to witness the proceedings, much to the disgust of Mr Humphries who had to 'carve his way through a wall of human flesh', to quote W. C. Fields. 'Bloody ghouls!' he said to himself as I drew near. 'Beg your pardon, Vicar,' he added as he breathed a whisky-laden aroma in my direction. 'Look at 'em, trampling over your gravestones and dropping confetti everywhere, watching another man going to his doom.'

'You had better be careful with your language, Mr Humphries,' I said to him. 'There's a bus-load of strict Baptists here from further up the valley, the bride's parents and friends.'

'That's all I need to know,' he replied. 'No glass of sherry at the reception in that case. Well, let's get on with it.' He pushed his way to the steps outside the church porch. 'Let's have a snap of the happy couple on their own first, shall we?'

Charles was carrying his father's top hat. He could not wear it because it was several sizes too large for him. When he tried it on in the vicarage, he was engulfed and resembled the illustration of the Mad Hatter in *Alice in Wonderland*.

When it came to the bride's family group, Mrs Williams was calling for the Reverend Josiah Jones-Evans to be included. A dapper little man, with a black trilby to match his black suit, appeared from the throng. Large horn-rimmed spectacles were perched on his beaky nose and evidently he had disdained to wear the obligatory white carnation which was available for guests of the family. By the sour look on his face, perhaps, the flower would have withered in his buttonhole. While everybody else attempted a 'cheese' smile, Josiah stood in splendid isolation, like death's head at the feast, obviously lamenting the desertion of one of his pet lambs to the Anglican fold.

As yet I had not met him. I pushed my way through the chaos to reach him as he stepped down from the family group.

'Mr Jones-Evans,' I gasped, 'I am Fred Secombe, the bridegroom's vicar.'

'Pleased to meet you,' he replied, without a trace of pleasure on his countenance. He deposited a limp right hand in my outstretched hand, withdrawing it in an instant as if he were fearful of being contaminated by the contact with an Anglican priest.

'Bronwen looks delightful, doesn't she?' I said. Small, dark-haired with large dark brown eyes, she reminded me of my wife on our wedding day. She had the same ready smile. 'We shall do our best to help her settle down to her new life. It will be a big change for her but with her good Christian background I am sure she will cope with her changed circumstances.'

'Changed circumstances!' exploded the Reverend Josiah, unable to contain himself any longer. 'With her dedication to her Saviour, the change in her circumstances should have meant her serving Him in a mission hospital in Africa, not wasting her life here in the valleys. She's too good to be spending her time drinking cups of tea with the Mothers' Union and darning the curate's socks. That child had a call, a real call, which has been deafened by the cotton-wool of an easy existence under the guise of serving the Lord in the comfort of a parsonage or a vicarage.'

The vehemence of this onslaught by the little man took my breath away. It was obvious that he must be a charismatic figure in his strict Baptist pulpit. It was also obvious that 'a few words' from the minister at the wedding reception would be disastrous.

'Well, Mr Jones-Evans,' I replied. 'I would have thought that it is only Bronwen who can judge whether a call is a real call or not. As far as I am concerned, I shall leave that judgement to her and her alone. If you will excuse me, I have to get to the hall to see that everything is ready for the reception.'

Before I left the church I had a brief word with my wife who was due to travel the short distance to the church hall in the same wedding car as the bridesmaids. I explained what had happened in my encounter with the minister. 'Why not ask him to say grace,' she suggested, 'and limit the speeches to the best man, the bride's father and yourself. If Mrs Williams doesn't like that, it is just too bad.'

When I arrived in the hall, the church Gilbert and Sullivan Society members were in a state of last-minute confusion, colliding with each other as they raced to place bread rolls on the plates and the condiments on the table, not to mention the delivery of wine glasses to contain the Wincarnis tonic wine for the toasts. The Society was one which I had created in my curate days in Pontywen. It was a benevolent dictatorship in which I acted as producer, director, tenor lead and policy-maker. Charles was the accompanist and my wife was the soprano lead. The musical director, Aneurin, had rehearsed an anthem with the members, Schubert's 'Ave Maria', which the *ad hoc* choir had sung impressively during the signing of the register. Now the choristers had become waiters and waitresses for the occasion.

'Vicar!' called Idris the Milk, churchwarden at St Padarn's, the daughter church in the parish, and a stalwart of the Society. 'Could I have a word with you, please?'

He took me by the arm and led me into the kitchen. 'We've got the bar in here if you want a drink – everything from whisky to a small barrel of beer. So if there's anybody who's allergic to Wincarnis, tell them to come into the kitchen and we'll put them right. How about a spot of scotch now before they all come in – build you up for your job as best man? By the look of that bus-load, you'll need it.'

'Thank you, Idris. I'll accept your offer but for heaven's sake don't let those Baptists see that you are serving strong drink. If they found that out, they would get up and walk out en masse.'

By the time I had swallowed a few mouthfuls of whisky, the guests were beginning to arrive. 'Here's a couple of peppermints, Vicar. Guaranteed to camouflage strong drink at a distance of inches. Suck those and you can look them in the eye without giving yourself away.' Idris produced a packet of mint humbugs from his pocket. 'Here you are! Keep the lot. Your need is greater than mine.'

I took two from the packet and stuffed the rest in my pocket. Sucking hard on the sweets, I went to meet Charles and Bronwen who had just made an appearance, followed closely by Bronwen's parents and the Reverend Josiah. I decided to take the bull by the horns. Taking the minister aside, I said to him, 'Would you like to say grace before the meal? I thought it would be appropriate if you had some part in the proceedings.'

He glared at me. 'Mrs Williams asked me if I would say a few words at the reception.'

'By saying grace, Mr Jones-Evans, you would be saying a few words. I could have asked the bridegroom's father or I could have said grace myself since I am the vicar. However, I am inviting you to say grace.'

His face reddened and he drew in his breath. He was silent for a few seconds. 'Very well,' he replied.

In the meanwhile Charles and Bronwen, with Mr and Mrs Williams plus a weary-looking Canon Wentworth-Baxter, were receiving their guests as they entered the hall. Eleanor and the two bridesmaids were engaged in earnest conversation near the table on which the wedding cake reposed as Humphries the Snap made his way towards me, carrying his photographic apparatus.

'Do you think I could have a snap of the bride and groom with the wedding cake before you all sit down for this meal?' he asked. 'I have another wedding at two o'clock and I'd like to get away if possible.'

'I'm sure you can,' I replied. 'By the way, if you go into

the kitchen, you'll find something much stronger than Wincarnis.'

I was sorry the moment I said it. I have never seen an old man move more quickly. He was in the kitchen before I could draw another breath. In the ten minutes or so that it took for the guests to be received, Mr Humphries had half emptied the whisky bottle, according to Idris. His abandoned tripod and camera stood forlornly in front of the wedding cake.

'Before we sit down for the meal, would you mind having your photograph taken, pretending to cut the wedding cake?' I said to Charles and Bronwen.

'Where is he?' asked Bronwen.

'I think he is in the kitchen. I'll go and get him. He'll be glad to get away.' He was not glad to get away.

'Can't they hold on for a minute or two, Vicar?'

'I think you had better come straight away. It was you who wanted to leave as quickly as possible. If you don't mind my saying so, you'll be in no fit condition to get to your next wedding unless you stop swigging that whisky.'

'Vicar! You insult me. I can always hold my liquor and my – er – speech is never shlurred.'

He poured half a tumbler of scotch down his throat and moved unsteadily into the hall.

The bride and groom were standing behind the three-tiered wedding cake, looking into each other's eyes.

'Would you mind standing at the side, please? I don't want to have a snap of the cake with a couple of heads peeping over the top.' He hiccuped and had difficulty getting under the cloth to take the photograph. It seemed that at any minute tripod camera and Mr Humphries would collapse on the church hall floor. Miraculously that disaster was averted, perhaps by the fervency of my prayer.

'Would you please stop moving about?' ordered the hidden photographer. Since Charles and Bronwen were standing perfectly still, holding the knife between them, they were somewhat bewildered by the remark. 'As far as I can tell, we are not moving at all,' said Charles.

'Right, that's fine. Now stay still.' A muffled hiccup was followed by the emergence from under his cover of Mr Humphries, whose tousled grey locks and bleary eyes, combined with his purple nose, would have made him an ideal subject for a comic postcard.

'Smile, please. Look at me, then. Come on. Let's shee your choppers.'

The bride and groom obliged with a display of their teeth more appropriate for a dental inspection than as an expression of happiness.

The camera shutter came down and their ordeal was over. The photographer made his unsteady way out of the hall, as I breathed a sigh of relief. I went over to Charles who was standing gazing into space while Bronwen was talking to her bridesmaid friends.

'That was a near squeak,' I said to him.

'What do you mean, Fred?' His childlike innocence was a constant source of amazement to me.

'Couldn't you see that he was squiffy, several sheets to the wind?'

He stared at me.

'Drunk, Charles. It's my fault. I told him that if he was allergic to Wincarnis he could get something stronger in the kitchen. I didn't realize that he could put away half a bottle of whisky in a matter of minutes.'

'You don't mean to say that they have drinks in the kitchen? What will that crowd of Baptists say?'

'That crowd of Baptists will not be invited into the kitchen, believe me. You did not expect the Gilbert and Sullivan crowd to go without the social lubricant on Easter Monday, did you? – Lent finished on Saturday. It is not an all-the-year-round exercise for us, even if it may be for them. What is more, I have a shrewd idea that if I invited your father-in-law into the kitchen he would come like a shot were it not for your mother-in-law. If you need a stiffener, I suggest you pop in there now before the proceedings begin.'

'I don't need anything of the sort. For heaven's sake, Fred, tell them in the kitchen to be careful. What if some of the Tabernacle lot go in there for a cup of tea or something and they find that they are boozing?'

'They won't find anything of the sort. I am positive that Idris the Milk who is in charge of the bar is far too discreet to let them know that Wincarnis and tea are not the only liquid available. I suggest that you collect

Bronwen and make your way to the top table. I am going to announce that the wedding breakfast is about to be served.'

I went into the kitchen where the girls were ready to move to the tables with plates of cold ham, tomatoes, lettuce and boiled potatoes. Idris was standing in a corner by the beer barrel. 'Before I borrow a spoon to bang on the table,' I said to him, 'Charles is desperate to let you know that he does not want any of the Tabernacle load to discover that there is illicit liquor on the premises. I told him that you would be the soul of discretion.'

'You know me, Vicar. I can guarantee that as far as this kitchen is concerned, the Baptists will think it is worthy of the Band of Hope.' With a nod and a wink, he handed me a large tablespoon. By now all the guests were seated. Mrs Williams was pouring out her soul to Canon Wentworth-Baxter, while Eleanor was engaged in animated conversation with Mr Williams. I banged loudly on the table and announced that the Reverend Josiah Jones-Evans would say grace. The little man was seated at the end of the top table.

'Will you all rise for the blessing on the food we are about to eat?' he ordered in a powerful pulpit voice. Chairs were noisily pushed backwards as the guests rose for the blessing. He waited for complete silence before launching into the longest grace I have ever heard.

'O Lord,' he began, 'we beseech you in your infinite wisdom and loving mercy to look down with your favour upon your children gathered around these tables and especially upon the two who have plighted their troth to each other. You know, all-seeing God, the secrets of our hearts and therefore why it is that Bronwen, your faithful servant, has chosen to turn from a dedicated life in the jungles of Africa to serve the sick in Pontywen and to share the life of a man of God in this town. May he realize the sacrifice of her dreams she has made for him and may he be worthy of that sacrifice. May God's blessing rest upon them and may that blessing also be upon his gracious gifts of food to be set before us. We ask this in the name of our Saviour, Jesus Christ.'

It was a *tour de force* which cast a blight upon the wedding feast. For the first few minutes afterwards there was an embarrassed silence, aggravated by a loud comment from Bertie Owen in the kitchen: 'That wasn't a grace. That was a sermon, and a rotten one too.' Bertie, former people's warden in St Padarn's until the people voted him out, was 'born to trouble as the sparks fly upward'.

'Shut up, Bertie,' hissed Idris the Milk.

'Only he could do that,' I whispered to Eleanor who was seated between me and Amos Williams. 'It's a wonder he didn't come out into the hall and confront Josiah.'

Bronwen was doing her best to comfort Charles whose face was scarlet throughout the meal. Her father concentrated on his food, looking to neither left nor right. Her mother tried to engage the canon in conversation but with little success. Meanwhile, the cause of the embarrassment was tucking into God's gifts with relish, content that he had used the grace to say his 'few words'.

Eventually, when the apple tart and custard had been consumed and the wine glasses were filled with the non-alcoholic wine, I read out the few telegrams and cards containing the best wishes for the happy couple.

That done, I turned to Mr Williams. 'Are you ready for your speech?' I asked.

'More than ready,' he muttered.

After he had been introduced, he sprang to his feet. 'Bride and groom, ladies and gentlemen. This should be a happy occasion. Our only child, my daughter Bronwen whom I love very dearly, is marrying the man she loves. What's more, I can see that he loves her just as deeply as she does him. She is not sacrificing any dream. I thank God that she is not out in a jungle in Africa, or anywhere else like that. There is plenty of good she can do here in the valleys and if she can do that, married to the man she loves, so much the better. She has been a joy to bring up, a pleasure to have in the house. I am sure that they both will be very happy now and in the years to come. Will you rise with me and drink a toast to the bride and groom? Charles and Bronwen.'

There was a smile on the faces of the happy couple for the first time since the meal began. There was a scowl on the face of the Reverend Josiah. As Amos Williams sat down, he said to me, 'I wish it could have been something stronger than Wincarnis.'

'Mr Williams,' I said, 'when the proceedings come to an end, I will take you to the kitchen where there is a stronger brew, more fitted to the occasion. After all, there was another wedding reception when water was turned into wine of the best quality. I think Charles and Bronwen are worthy of a toast in the best drink available.'

'Hear, hear,' he replied. 'In that case, hurry up and get the speeches over so that we can go and indulge – but for heaven's sake keep my missus out of the kitchen.'

When I called on Charles to reply to the toast, he whispered to me that he was going to cut it short. 'Thank you, father-in-law, for that splendid speech, and thank you both for producing such a wonderful daughter. I can assure you that I will love and cherish her as I promised in the marriage service. I can also assure the Reverend Josiah Jones-Evans that she is already giving dedicated service to the patients in Pontywen Hospital who need her loving care as much as any patients in Africa or wherever.' His voice was raised in anger as he spoke those words. He paused to recover his self-control. 'I should like to thank Mr and Mrs Williams for this reception and, of course, my friends in the Gilbert and Sullivan Society for all their kind help and also for the lovely anthem in the service. Will you please join me in a toast to the lovely bridesmaids and to the equally lovely matron of honour?'

A loud burst of applause came from the kitchen staff when Charles sat down to be greeted by a kiss from his bride. The Reverend Josiah's head was bowed as he examined his empty plate.

As I rose to speak, I felt that it would be unwise to add to the minister's discomfort. 'On behalf of the lovely bridesmaids and of course the delicious matron of honour' (Eleanor gave me one of her remonstrative looks) 'I should like to thank the bridegroom for his compliments and the brevity of his eloquence. I shall be equally brief. It is some three years more or less since Charles first came to this parish as my fellow curate. I can say in all honesty that he has been a good friend and is now developing into a good parish priest. He is full of the unexpected. Bronwen will find that life with him will never be boring – the secret of a good marriage. He is fortunate to have such a good Christian girl as Bronwen as his partner. She will grace any parsonage or vicarage which will come their way in the future. May God bless them both and may they always be as happy as they are today.'

After I had announced that no more speeches were to be given, I invited Amos Williams to follow me into the kitchen. 'What would you like? A scotch or a beer?' I asked.

'A large scotch would be more than welcome,' he replied.

When Idris the Milk had handed the bride's father a generous helping of whisky, I whispered to the bar-tender, 'Keep an eye open for Mrs Williams. If she finds him imbibing, there will be trouble.'

'Turn around, Vicar. It looks as if there is trouble coming from a different quarter. Here comes Will Book and Pencil,' said Idris.

I looked out through the kitchen window to see PC Will Davies standing at the back of the hall. His excessive devotion to duty had earned him his nickname and a reputation of being unbearably officious.

I left the kitchen and went across to the constable who was making his way into the middle of the hall.

'Well, PC Davies,' I said. 'What can we do for you?'

'You realize, Vicar, that you cannot serve intoxicating drinks in your hall without a licence?' He gave me his best magisterial stare.

'I am afraid, Constable, that you have come on a fruitless mission if you think that the guests have been served any strong drink. Since the bride's parents are Baptist and most of the wedding party are Baptists, the wine glasses were filled with Wincarnis tonic wine for the toasts. If you care to inspect the glasses, you can see for yourself.'

His face was a picture of thwarted authority.

'I take your word for it, Vicar, as a man of the cloth. I wouldn't have come here but for the fact that I found Mr

Hubert Humphries, the photographer, sitting on a wall near Pontywen Methodist Church, drunk and incapable with his apparatus. He said he was on his way to take photographs at a wedding in that church and that he had just come from a reception in your church hall. They have had to take photographs with their own cameras at the Methodists'. He must have called in somewhere on his way, I suppose. Sorry to have troubled you.'

'Before you go, PC Davies,' I said, 'I think you will find that we could have served intoxicating liquor in this church hall, as long as no one purchased it. I suggest that next time you intrude upon an occasion such as this you read up the relevant legislation beforehand. It will save you and others a lot of trouble.'

'What you call the biter bit,' remarked Idris, as the embarrassed policeman left the hall. 'Well done, Vicar. Come and join Mr Williams for a spot of the hard stuff. That was something worth celebrating.'

'Too late, Idris, by the look of it. Mrs Williams has just invaded the kitchen. I think Mr Williams will have other things on his mind.'

'I have some very interesting news for you, Vicar,' announced my wife when she returned from her surgery at lunch-time. 'Your curate is due to become a father at the end of the year.' It was some two months or so after the eventful wedding.

'Bronwen presented herself for examination this morning. Without a shadow of a doubt she is well and truly preggers. It must be a honeymoon child. If so, they are certainly paying for their pleasure. At least, the blushing bride thinks so.'

'You mean she doesn't want the child?'

'Oh, she wants to have a child, but not so soon. She will be washing nappies before she has time to get the confetti out of her hair. Apparently she has not told Charles yet.'

'Obviously not. He was his new carefree self this morning at Matins. I wonder what his reaction will be. I can't imagine him as a father. I know one thing. When she has labour pains he will be having them with her and his pains will be greater than hers. I can see the doctor having two patients on his hands in the maternity hospital.'

'She wants to have the baby at home and she wants me to deliver it. In that case you will have to be his doctor. I shall be far too preoccupied with Bronwen to bother with him.'

He needed my patient care the very next morning at

Matins when he arrived at church looking as if he was in imminent danger of a nervous collapse. There were dark circles under his eyes as if he had not slept all night.

'Has Eleanor told you the news?' he said as soon as he came into the vestry. He spoke as if he had been visited by the Black Death. 'Who would have thought it?'

'Congratulations, Charles. You must be a very proud man. You have beaten me to it and by several lengths at that.'

He stared at me as if I were someone bereft of his senses. 'It's not fair,' he moaned. 'We have hardly had any time together and now there will be three of us in the house. It means that Bronwen will have to give up her job at the hospital and we shall have to manage on my stipend. There's no need to tell you how much that is.'

'There are just two things to say in answer to that. I suppose you know what causes babies. If you don't, Bronwen certainly does. If you didn't want to have a family just yet, there are precautions you could have taken to ensure that the increase in your family could have waited a while. Secondly, Charles, you are about to become a father, one of the greatest privileges life can offer. You will find you will be able to manage financially until Bronwen is ready to go back to her nursing. For heaven's sake, man, cheer up. This is not the end of the world. It is the beginning of a new one.'

'Don't get me wrong, Fred. Of course I shall be proud to be a father and especially since Bronwen will be the mother of my child. It's just that she isn't all that strong and I don't want anything to go wrong with the birth.'

'That's a fine thing to say to the husband of the doctor who is going to take care of your wife. As far as I can find out from Eleanor, she is perfectly well and will be in good condition to deliver a child. In any case, if anything appears to be amiss, then I am sure that my wife will see that she goes into hospital and has the expert attention of a consultant. Now, is there anything else you want to say to justify your totally unreasonable attitude to the birth of your child? Bronwen will need all the support that you can give her. I hope you greeted the news from her with enthusiasm, even if you had to manufacture it.'

'I'm sorry, Fred. I'm afraid I was not over-enthusiastic. If it comes to that, neither was she. I promise that I will give her all the support she needs.'

'My dear Charles, as the weeks go by, the truth will dawn on you that you have been blessed, not cursed. You will find that as the time draws near for the birth of the baby, you will get more and more excited. Now, come on, let's go in and say our prayers. That will help you to a true perspective.'

As we went into the church to say our prayers, I felt I had to pray fervently for Bronwen who would have two children by the end of the year. The one with the nappy would be easier to manage than the other.

When I told Eleanor later in the day of his reaction, she said, 'I am not at all surprised. Charles is a very selfish person and he can see that the baby will be a rival for the affection of his beloved Bronwen. What is more, it means that she will have less time to prepare his meals and to iron his shirts and trousers. All we can do is to give them both as much help as possible.'

'By the way,' I replied, 'he said that Bronwen is not all that strong and he did not want anything to go wrong with the birth.'

'Let me tell you this, Frederick. That girl is much stronger than he is. She may be small but physically she will be able to bear a child without any trouble at all. Make no mistake about that. If he were in her position he would not be able to produce a mouse, let alone a child. He would have died of fright when the pains came on. As for anything going wrong with the birth, if there were the slightest indication I should make sure that the best available consultant would be on hand.'

'Those were my exact words, my love, when he mentioned it. I know one thing, he will be suffering from nervous headaches and stomach-aches for the next seven months.'

They began the very next day when he failed to appear at Matins. There had been a complete transformation in his daily pattern after his engagement to Bronwen. He was punctual for all the services and active in the parish. Now I would be hearing one of his favourite phrases, 'Sorry for the lapse, Fred,' repeated several times in the course of the coming months.

All thoughts of Charles and his fatherhood future were quickly dispelled when I returned to the vicarage after morning service. Standing on the doorstep was Councillor David Waters, known to the Pontywen populace as 'Dai Spout'. Resplendent in his black suit, trilby and his shining black boots, he presented a picture of pomposity writ large.

'Good morning, Vicar,' he proclaimed in his best oratorical tones. 'I thought I would catch you when you returned from your service. I wonder if you could spare me some of your precious time.'

'By all means, Councillor Waters. Come on in. I have to take a sick communion at half past ten but I am free until then. Perhaps you would like a cup of tea or a cup of coffee.'

'A cup of tea would suit me nicely. The people's drink.'

'As you please, Councillor. I suppose it depends upon who the people are.'

'Very funny, Vicar,' he said, and followed me into the vicarage.

I decided to take him into the study where I could sit behind my big desk. I wondered why he was being obsequious in his approach to me. Perhaps a little show of power complex on my part would not go amiss. I ushered him into the leather armchair in front of the desk and went into the kitchen to make the tea. When I returned, he was standing up, examining the contents of my bookshelves.

'I see you've got books by William Temple here. You know he was President of the Workers' Educational Association at one time? Great man, great socialist. Pity he died so soon after becoming Archbishop of Canterbury.'

'A great pity. He was a wonderful man.'

I was not going to rise to the bait and declare my political preferences. I felt that I should not make public my allegiance to any party.

'Milk and sugar, Councillor?' I said.

'Not much milk and two spoonfuls, thank you. Nice study you've got here, Vicar. The last time I was in it was when we came to put the banns in for our wedding. Chapel I am, but the wife is Church, as you know. I'm glad my son is getting confirmed next month. I'm all for the youngsters getting a good grounding in Christianity. My trouble is I've had too busy a time with the party on Sundays to be able to go to church. We have all our committee meetings on Sunday mornings. Anyway, I haven't come here to waste your time. So I'll come straight to the point, as it were. I don't know whether you've heard or not but the council has done me the honour of asking me to be mayor at the end of next month. I should have asked you some time ago, but what with one thing and another ... you know how it is. Anyway, I would be very pleased if you would agree to be my chaplain for my year of office.'

As he swallowed his first mouthful of tea, I sat back in my chair and examined the desk, trying to come to terms with the unexpected. Before I could reply, the councillor launched into a job description of the chaplain's duties.

'Let me explain what is involved, Vicar. There would be a civic service here in St Mary's when you would preach the sermon. This would come after the mayor-making at which you would be present. Then the chaplain has to say prayers before each monthly meeting of the Council. Occasionally you would accompany me to various functions – and that's about it. Your good lady wife, Dr Secombe, would be invited to these of course, if she is able to be present. I know what a busy life she has and if she could not attend some of the functions, we would understand. Well, there it is in a nutshell, as it were.'

'It is quite a big nutshell, Councillor Waters, I must say. Thank you very much for inviting me to be your chaplain. It is an honour which I accept. I am afraid that my wife will have to miss some of the functions because of her duties. However, she will be having a partner to join her in the practice next week and accordingly she will have more free time available.'

He stood up and extended his right hand.

'Thank you, Vicar, for accepting this office for the coming year.' He shook my hand warmly. 'I shall look forward to your company. My wife will be very pleased. Well, I had better be off now. I have to get all the arrangements made for my installation, as it were. Perhaps you will let me know what hymns and readings you will be having in the civic service so that we can get everything in hand at the printers. I'll get the mayor's secretary to send you a copy of last year's service to give you some idea of what is involved, as it were.'

As we strolled down the vicarage drive, I wondered how many 'as it were's' I would hear over the next twelve months.

Half an hour later, after a protracted, one-sided conversation with our loquacious daily help, Mrs Watkins, who had arrived just after Dai Spout had left, I made my way to Miss Agnew to bring her the sacrament. Florence Agnew was an elderly spinster whose father had been an archdeacon in Mid Wales. She was a tall, thin lady who spent her waking hours wandering about the ground floor of her large red-brick house, The Knoll, clad in her nightdress and dressing-gown. Her fingers were all bound in sticking plaster and she reeked of brandy. My monthly communion visit to her entailed a quarter of an hour's service and a minimum of an hour's conversation, equally as one-sided as that with Mrs Watkins, but decidedly more interesting. Miss Agnew was a much-travelled lady with tales to tell from the days of the Raj to the heyday of the Kaiser's Germany, with picture albums and illustrations. Eleanor informed me that the sticking plaster on the fingers was quite unnecessary but was one of the badges of her eccentricity.

I had to wait the usual few minutes in the porch after ringing the doorbell. The grass in Miss Agnew's front garden was as high as an elephant's eye and there had

24

been an invasion of thistles into cracks in the concrete path to the front door. When the door was opened, the bouquet of her brandy caressed my nostrils as Miss Agnew bade me good morning. Her long, straggling white hair was cascaded over the shoulders of her navy-blue dressing-gown.

'Come on in, Vicar,' she croaked, and swayed gently ahead of me into the spacious drawing-room where on a table in the bay window reposed a wooden cross in the centre of a spotless white cloth. 'I've got everything ready for you.' She cleared her throat. 'I'm afraid my voice is a little husky this morning. It must be this dry weather. I am trying to keep my throat moist. You must excuse me if my participation in the service is somewhat muffled.'

'Not to worry, Miss Agnew. I'm sure the Lord will hear your every word.'

She eased herself into an armchair at the side of the table and opened the prayer-book which lay on its arm. 'It is the first Sunday after Trinity, this week's Epistle and Gospel, isn't it?'

'It is indeed.'

'I love the Epistle with its message that God is love. When I was a child that was the text which used to be above my bed. It was beautifully embroidered, I wonder where it went. After my father's death when my mother had to move out of the rectory, she disposed of so much because she had to move into a smaller house. That was one of the things that went.'

By now I was ready to begin the service. Every time I came to The Knoll she provided me with a memory recall as an accompaniment to my robing and the preparation of the elements – it was part of the ritual.

The service over, she remained silent in her armchair,

her head bowed, as I cleansed the vessels of my pocket communion set which she had given me when I first came to give her communion.

'Haven't you your own little set like Canon Llewellyn and Father Whittaker?' she had asked. They were my predecessors and had spent many more years in the ministry than I. When I came next to give her communion, there was a parcel on the table with its white cloth and its wooden cross. Inside was an expensive pocket communion set and a card bearing the inscription: 'May we celebrate together the Lord's Supper many more times in the future, Florence Agnew'.

As I took off my surplice and stole, she looked up at me from her armchair, with a wicked glint in her eye, after receiving the holy sacrament.

'Now then, Vicar, would you care for a small brandy and a coffee while we have our tête-à-tête?' It was always the same question. It was always the same reply.

'If you will allow me to make the coffee, Miss Agnew, while you pour the brandy, I shall be delighted.'

The coffee percolator was bubbling merrily when I went into the kitchen. Two coffee cups were waiting to be filled. On the tray, together with the delicate china and sugar bowl, was a plate of cream biscuits.

When I entered the drawing-room bearing the refreshments, the 'small brandy' on a little side-table by the armchair I was to occupy, was half-way up a large brandy glass.

For an hour I listened to Miss Agnew's description of Bavaria in the first decade of the twentieth century. She had a great love of Nuremberg and had made some excellent charcoal sketches of the medieval square below the Kaiser, the imperial castle which dominates the town.

There was Albrecht Dürer's house and an impressive portrayal of the west front of the famous Frauenkirche with its mechanical clock. 'And to think that this lovely city was defiled by that perverted little Austrian for his dreadful rallies in the thirties,' she said bitterly. 'Next time you come I must show you drawings I made of the Passion Play at Oberammergau and of the town of Augsburg.'

As I came down from the hillside where Miss Agnew's house was perched overlooking the town, Nuremberg and its splendour were forgotten when I came back to the reality of 1948 in Pontywen in the person of Bertie Owen who had been a thorn in my flesh ever since I had come to Pontywen. He had been people's warden at St Padarn's for many years until he was voted out of office at the Easter Vestry a year ago. A shop steward at the steelworks, he had carried his imperious attitude into his church activities, only to alienate the bulk of the congregation.

He crossed the road in Balaclava Street, and stood in my path. 'Vicar, just the man I want to see.'

Bertie was the last man I wanted to see.

'What can I do for you, Bertie?' I should have said that I was in a hurry and had to get back to the vicarage. It would have saved me five minutes and a great deal of the unnecessary worry that followed.

'I don't want to be talking like this to you in the street, but it's about Albert Williams.'

'What about Albert Williams, Bertie?'

He looked around the empty street as if it were full of eavesdroppers. Then he came close up to me and spoke in hushed tones. 'He's getting far too friendly with the choir-boys at St Padarn's, some of them have been going round to his house in the evenings.'

Albert Williams was a bachelor who had become the organist at the daughter church, some six months previously. He was a pleasant young man, who worked in the local bank having been excused National Service because he suffered from a mild form of epilepsy called 'petit mal'. Albert had done wonders for the music of St Padarn's and had recruited several boys whom he was training to a high standard of vocal ability. In so doing he had aroused jealousy among the middle-aged and elderly ladies of the choir who felt that they were being pushed into the background. Foremost among them was Agnes Collier, widow of the former organist, and leading soprano soloist for the past thirty years. Somewhat effeminate, Albert was the butt of many remarks from the entire female complement about the 'pansy's' lack of manliness.

'Do you realize, Bertie, that you are making serious allegations without a shred of evidence? At least, I assume that's the case. Has any choir-boy said that anything untoward has happened at his house? In any case, it is not his house, as you know. It is his mother's house and I am sure that would be sufficient guarantee that the boys were there for one purpose only and that is to have their voices trained – something Albert is doing to great effect.'

Bertie's ruddy countenance deepened in colour.

'All I know, Vicar, is that Agnes Collier happened to be passing his place the other night and saw through the window that he had his arm around young David Morris.'

'Agnes Collier had better keep her suspicions to herself. If that is the only evidence she can provide for a very nasty slur on Albert's reputation, she should be ashamed of herself. So should you, Bertie, for passing on such poisonous gossip.'

He began to bluster. 'I was just doing my duty. I thought you should know what was being said. You are the vicar of the parish, after all.'

'Well, as vicar of the parish, I warn you that if I hear any more of this poisonous gossip I shall have to report it to Albert Williams, giving him the names of those responsible for it. Then if he wants to take action against them he can do so. If you will excuse me, Bertie, I have to get back to the vicarage, otherwise I shall be late for lunch.'

When I arrived at the vicarage, Eleanor was back from her rounds and was about to put a parcel of fish and chips in the oven.

'Just in time, love. Fresh from Cascarini's. Two hake cutlets and sixpenn'orth of chips.' As she bent down to put our meal in the oven I gave her a pat on her posterior.

'You naughty vicar,' she said. 'What's that for?'

'Miss Agnew's brandy has inflamed my passions, I am afraid.'

'Don't be afraid, Frederick, but keep them bottled up until this evening for a more convenient time.'

'By the way, my sweet. I have news for you that will make a lunch of fish and chips look very infra dig. Soon we shall be invited to three-course luncheons with wine to wash them down and to the occasional five-course dinner in the evening with even more exotic refreshments.'

'Explain yourself, please. Whence come the invitations to these shindigs?'

'Well, this morning Dai Spout appeared on the doorstep when I came back from Matins, which was curateless, as we expected.'

'Never mind about that! Come to the point, Secombe.'

'"In a nutshell, as it were", to quote the worthy Councillor, he has asked me to be his chaplain for his year of office which begins next month.'

'That's very short notice, Fred. Perhaps he has asked somebody else who has turned him down.'

'It is the end of next month and apparently he had been thinking of asking me but kept putting it off. Most likely because he had a conscience about his non church-going.'

'More than likely. Congratulations, but you realize that it puts an end to our Gilbert and Sullivan participation for the next twelve months.'

'I realize that. The only thing I can do is to have a word with Aneurin. Apparently the English teacher who produces the school play is an accomplished stage director. As for our roles as Marco and Gianetta I am sure we can find replacements. Iorweth Ellis will be only too pleased to take over my part. He will be able to sing it but the stage director will have his work cut out to turn him into an actor. Perhaps Aneurin knows of some experienced soprano who will "do" Gianetta.'

'I suppose it is just as well. What with my new National Health Service commitments and coping with a new partner in the practice, I think I shall have enough on my plate. There will be occasions when I shall not find it possible to come to some of those luncheons you talked about. I shall make sure I manage the dinners.'

As we were eating our fish and chips I mentioned my confrontation with Bertie about Albert Williams.

'That is typical of Agnes Collier. No wonder her best friends address her as "Ag". The trouble about that kind of talk is the comment it draws from the ignorant that "There's no smoke unless there's fire." Do you think you should have a word with Albert about it? Perhaps it would be better if he confined his voice training to the Church chancel. He is such an effeminate young man that anything he does with young boys will give rise to gossip, for the slightest reason.'

'Perhaps I'll do that but it will have to be a passing reference in the vestry or at the organ. If I pay a visit to his home it will make him think that he is the centre of talk in the church. That would mean his resignation and we shall have lost a very good organist and choir-master.'

After lunch I decided to call on Charles – not only to find out why he was not at service that morning but to check whether he had heard the rumour that Bertie Owen had passed on to me. Bronwen opened the door to me when I rang the doorbell. She seemed surprised to see me.

'Charles left here about half an hour ago to see you at the vicarage. I was on early shift at the hospital and left him in bed. Apparently he overslept. He came to the vicarage later on but you were not in. I have given him a good talking-to about slipping back into his old ways. Whether it will do any good or not, I really don't know.'

'Thank you for your support, Bronwen. I shall reinforce what you said to him when I see him. I think I had better do some hospital visiting now. Perhaps you would ask him to come and see me about six o'clock before Eleanor and I have our meal, that is, if it doesn't clash with your arrangements.'

'Certainly not. We shall be eating at five o'clock. I shall see that he is fed and watered by six.'

Promptly at six o'clock Charles was on my doorstep, looking suitably chastened, with his puppy-dog look much in evidence.

'Sorry for the lapse, Fred. I have been here twice to

apologize. First this morning, then this afternoon. I would have been here earlier and would have caught you before you went out but I was held up on my way here. As a matter of fact I would like a few words with you about that.'

'Come on in, you reprobate. I thought the leopard had got rid of his spots. Evidently I was wrong.'

We went into my study as the appetizing odour of Eleanor's cooking began to percolate through the open door of the kitchen.

Before I could sit down in my favourite chair behind my desk, he launched into an elaborate apology, blaming his sleepless night for his late rising and assuring me that it was a one-off hiccup in his regeneration.

'All right, Charles, I am willing to accept the apology, but let me emphasize that if it is the beginning of a slide into your former habits you will have to start looking elsewhere for another curacy. Now then, what about the few words about being held up on your way here?'

'I had got as far as Mafeking Street when I met Mrs Morris – you know, David Morris's mother – the choir-boy in St Padarn's.'

My heart began to sink.

'It seems that young David has been going round to Albert Williams' home for some voice-training. She doesn't mind that – but the last couple of times he has been there he has been coming home at half past nine to ten o'clock. When she asks David why he has been so late, he says that they have been listening to classical music on his radiogram. She says if it happens again, she will have to take David out of the choir.'

'And I thought it was just Agnes Collier,' I said.

3

Albert Williams was a rosy-cheeked, bespectacled young man, immaculately dressed, who gave the impression that he had not yet begun to shave, even at the age of twenty-two. His mother, a widow, had been the school nurse until she retired in 1939. Albert was her only child, born to her when she was in her early forties. Her husband Reginald had been a clerk in the rates office and was known locally as Reg the Spats because of his penchant for that item of dress. He had died at the outbreak of the war, only weeks before Henrietta's retirement. Since then Albert had been the victim of what old Canon Llewellyn had termed 'smother love'. He had no school-friends and his leisure time was devoted to the piano and his Raleigh bicycle on which he was accompanied by his mother on the machine which had taken her around the schools in the Pontywen area. At weekends they would be seen riding out into the rural scenery which lay beyond the town.

They lived in a small semi-detached house in Ashburnham Close, one of the few non-terraced streets in Pontywen. Nurse Williams, as she was known to the local inhabitants, was a regular attendant at the parish church, and Albert had been a member of the choir since his early boyhood. After the sudden death of Mr Collier, the organist at St Padarn's Church, there was a hiatus which a volunteer organist, Miss Usher, filled inadequately. Albert had been practising on the organ at the parish church for some years and acted as a very accomplished deputy to Mr Greenfield, the regular organist. After some weeks of Miss Usher, I felt that the congregation at St Padarn's deserved better than her thud and blunder. Accordingly I invited Albert to take over as organist and choirmaster in the daughter church. In a few weeks there was a marked improvement in the quality of the music and in no time at all there were six extra choir-boys. It was a success story bitterly resented by Mrs Agnes Collier, who could see her soloist status of thirty years' standing being usurped by young David Morris, the leading choir-boy.

After Charles's encounter with Mrs Morris I decided to abandon my idea of a casual remark in the vestry or the chancel and instead to have a word with Albert at his home. 'The sooner the better in that case,' suggested Eleanor. 'Otherwise you have the making of a scandal which will damage St Padarn's much more than Miss Usher's dreadful organ-playing. Why not go this evening after dinner?'

As I entered Ashburnham Close, there was the sound of lawn-mowers at work in the dying sunshine. Expensive cars were parked in the drives. At the end of the cul-de-sac was the little three-up and three-down house with its neighbour, the only 'semis' in a small road of detached residences housing the elite of Pontywen from the manager of the steelworks to the owner of the local bus company. I pushed open the green wooden gate which bore the name 'Chatsworth' on the metal plate nailed to its top. The little lawn was immaculately mown and in its centre was a flower-bed featuring three standard rose trees with buds ready to burst into bloom. From inside the house piano music could be faintly heard.

By the time I had rung the doorbell, I was beginning to regret my instant decision to confront Albert. The appearance of his stern-faced mother at the door did little to help my rapidly diminishing self-confidence. She had always been a martinet in the clinics and was even more so at home.

'Good evening, Vicar!' she said, showing no sign of pleasure at my appearance. 'What brings you here at this time of night?' Considering that it was only half past eight, it was not an auspicious start to my errand.

'I have come to have a chat with Albert about the – er – music in St Padarn's.'

'There's nothing wrong with it, I hope,' she snapped.

'Not at all. On the contrary, it is very good, excellent, in fact.'

On hearing that, she invited me in. Albert was in the middle of a loud passage in a Chopin sonata and she had to tap twice on the door of the front room before he heard her knock. He stopped playing and shouted, 'What is it, Mother? Am I playing too loudly?'

'The vicar is here to see you.' With that she opened the door and ushered me in.

'Vicar! What an unexpected pleasure,' said the young man. 'Take a pew, as you might say.'

'I'll leave you two then to your business.' So saying, his mother disappeared into the back part of the house.

I sat down in an armchair near the window. He left the piano stool and sat opposite me in the other armchair.

'Sorry to interrupt your Chopin, Albert. I suppose it was Chopin, by the way?'

'Oh yes, it was Chopin. One of his polonaises, no. 53. I enjoy playing those compositions. A lot of his patriotism went into them.'

'Very interesting.' I said. 'I was somewhat wary about identifying the composer, having learned a lesson from the warden of my college. Two students would be invited for coffee with that important gentleman every Sunday evening to listen to a weekly music recital on the wireless. My friend and I were his guests on one occasion. He turned on the set just after the piano music had begun. A few minutes later, in a break between the movements, he said to us, "I do love Chopin." A quarter of an hour later, as the performance ended, the announcer informed us that the composer was Beethoven. The warden didn't turn a hair. "Now then," he said, "shall we have some coffee after that beautiful Beethoven?" I am afraid I could never do that. I should want to find the nearest hole to bury myself. That is why I could never become warden of a college, amongst other drawbacks on my part.'

'You mentioned coffee, Vicar. Would you care for a cup of coffee?'

'No, thank you. I have just come from drinking two cupfuls at the vicarage. In any case I don't want to interrupt your enjoyment of the polonaises for too long. I have just popped in to have a word about young David Morris.'

His face paled.

'It seems that his mother told Mr Wentworth-Baxter that unless he comes home earlier from his voice training with you, she will have to take him from the choir. I thought you ought to know, especially since he is such a gifted boy soprano.'

The colour began to return to his countenance.

'He is a very promising lad and his voice is of cathedral quality. It would be a tragedy to lose him. I suppose it is my fault – I have been encouraging a love of music in him by playing classical stuff, orchestral and vocal, on the radiogram and that has made him rather late leaving here. You can tell Mrs Morris that I shall see he is home early from now on.'

'If you don't mind me saying so, it would be wiser if you confined your voice training to the chancel. In that way there would be no come-back from Mrs Morris or anybody else.'

'What do you mean by "anybody else", Vicar? I hope no one has been suggesting that there has been something going on in my relationship with David Morris or any other choir-boy, come to that. If that is so I had better resign and finish with it.'

'Now, calm down, Albert, and stop talking about resigning. That would make it appear that something had been "going on", as you put it. You are doing a splendid job with the choir. It would be a great pity if that came to a stop. I am simply saying that choir practice is best carried on in the church, including individual tuition or whatever.'

He was silent for a while. Then he turned around and faced me.

'I suppose you are right, Vicar. I know very well what some of those old dears in the choir are like. From now on, I shall keep to the church premises for all my practices and voice training – then nobody can say anything.'

'Very wise, Albert. Now I'll leave you to get on with your Chopin.' We shook hands and he saw me to the door.

As I was about to close the gate, I looked up and saw his mother peering out of the bedroom window from behind a curtain. I wondered whether I should have told him to say nothing to her about the purpose of my visit.

I mentioned this to Eleanor when I returned to the vicarage. 'You can't very well tell a son to keep confidences from his mother, Fred. I expect she was straight down the stairs as soon as you had left to find out what happened. By the way, I find it strange that she knocked on the door of the front room to get permission to enter. It is not at all like her to do that. I'm sure it is just as well that you have ended this front-room session with David Morris in view of that. Perhaps young Albert is not as much under his mother's thumb as we had thought.'

Next morning I had a visit from Mr Victor Thomas, the diocesan secretary of the Church of England Men's Society. He was a bombastic gentleman, short, rotund, with dark hair, plastered with brilliantine and parted down the middle. He wore large horn-rimmed spectacles and sported a carefully manicured slimline moustache. A pair of spats adorned the top of his shiny black shoes beneath his immaculate black pin-stripe suit. He carried his Anthony Eden trilby in his hand.

'Ah, Vicar. I hoped I might catch you in. I should have made an appointment, I know, but I happened to be in the vicinity and took a chance. I wonder if I might have a word with you about the CEMS. I shall only keep you a few minutes.' I had heard about Victor's 'five minutes', which could over-run by half an hour at least.

'Come on in, Mr Thomas, I can only give you a few minutes anyway. I have to go to an important meeting at the town hall.' The important meeting was simply to hand in the order of service I had compiled to the mayor's secretary.

Mr Thomas was suitably impressed. 'Of course, you are to be the new mayor's chaplain, aren't you? Quite an honour, Vicar.'

'I don't know about that. The one thing I do know is that the next twelve months will be very busy for me.'

He made himself comfortable in the armchair opposite the desk in my study, as if he was fully prepared to multiply 'the few minutes'.

'Well,' he said, making an expansive gesture with his left hand, 'I suppose you could call this an important meeting. I have been looking up the records and I find that you had a branch of CEMS in this parish some twenty years ago, until it was closed down by the late Canon Llewellyn. With all the men returning from the Forces, our committee is planning a big drive to attract them to the Church – just the right time to revive the branch in your parish.'

His whole attitude and appearance riled me. 'And what are to be the attractions to bring men hardened by the war into the Church?' The tone of my voice opened his eyes wide behind his horn-rimmed glasses. He began to stammer a reply.

'Oh – er, we are putting together a list of speakers on interesting topics. For example, we have just persuaded the headmaster of one of the grammar schools to join our panel. He is going to talk about the origin of place-names in South Wales. We've got an ornithologist to give an illustrated lecture on rare birds, and so on. Then, of course, we have our big rally at the Cathedral once a year.'

'I am told, Mr Thomas, that you always manage to arrange it on Cup Final day when most men will be glued to their wireless sets.'

'You've got to have a sense of priority, Vicar. A rally at the Cathedral is much more important than the Cup Final.'

'I am sorry, but I shall certainly not "revive" the branch in this parish. If it had been a live one, Canon Llewellyn would not have closed it down. On the other hand I am thinking of organizing a men's club, with their own club tie. It will meet in the back room of a pub where they can listen to a speaker on some really interesting topic with a pint in their hands instead of a lukewarm cup of tea in a draughty church hall. We could arrange club outings and an occasional cricket match. I think that will be a better way to attract men into the church in Pontywen than your way of doing it.'

He lay back in the armchair with his mouth open, apparently searching for words which refused to come out. After a brief pause he recovered his wits and launched into an attack upon me. 'Well, Vicar, I must say your attitude shocks me. Yes, "shock" is the word. To think of substituting the public house for the church hall. Well, I must say. Whatever next! I suppose before long you will be advocating church services in public houses. I can only hope that none of the other younger clergy follow your example. It will be God help our churches if they do. Good morning, Vicar.'

Mr Victor Thomas spat the word 'Vicar' and was out of the study before I could show him to the door. As he strode up the drive, I noticed his trilby by the armchair. Opening the study window, I shouted, 'Mr Thomas, you have forgotten your hat.' He came to a halt as quickly as a Welsh guardsman on parade and stood facing the vicarage gate. I picked up his hat and dashed to the front door which he had left open, to find him still standing, but now in an about-turn position, waiting to receive his precious trilby. He glared at me and snapped a 'thank you'. I caught hold of his arm. 'Shall we at least shake hands, Mr Thomas?' I asked. 'I'm sorry if I offended you but at least you know where I stand now.' I offered him my right hand which he seemed to regard with suspicion. After a pause he put a limp hand into mine and then withdrew it as quickly as possible. He said no more but turned on his heels, rammed his hat on his head and disappeared into Church Street. I was never troubled with him again, unlike most of my fellow incumbents.

When I returned to the study, I sat at my desk, thinking over the idea of a men's club. The name is going to be important, I said to myself, something snappy and easily remembered. We had not long finished celebrating the centenary of St Mary's Church. Why not something connected with that? It could hardly be called the Centenary Club, but what about – the Centurion's Club? The more I thought about it, the more attractive it sounded.

By the time Mrs Watkins, our daily, had prepared lunch, I had formulated a programme of activities, and decided on a suitable venue, the Prince of Wales on the outskirts of Pontywen. The landlord, Jim Pritchard, was a nominal churchman and moreover the pub had a large meeting room at the back which was used for rehearsals by the Pontywen Silver Band. When Eleanor arrived after her stint of home visits, I was all set to launch into details of the new club, but the look of distress on her face as she came in the house put an end to that.

'What's the matter, love?' I asked. 'You look as if you have had some kind of a shock.'

'I suppose you could say that. Let's get in the house and I'll tell you all about it. I think a snort of whisky is called for.'

We went into the sitting-room where I poured her a large scotch with one for myself. 'This one is just to keep you company,' I said.

Her face relaxed for a moment. 'Aren't you glad I needed a stimulant, Frederick?' She collapsed into an armchair. 'Well,' she went on, 'you will be surprised to know that my intended partner in the practice has written to me at the surgery to say that he will not be joining me next week or any other week. He has been offered a much more lucrative post in the posh part of Cardiff. It came out of the blue, he says. He apologizes for letting me down but hopes that I shall soon find somebody else to fill the gap. What am I going to do, Fred? Now that the National Health Service has started, we have been snowed under with patients wanting to join the practice, as you know. The paperwork alone is mountainous. What am I to do?'

'I think the first thing you have to do is to give your father a ring,' I said firmly. Eleanor's father was a doctor in practice further up the Valley in delightfully rural surroundings, and serving a prosperous little market town. An ex-miner, he adored his daughter, an only child, of whom he was inordinately proud, unlike his wife who came from a middle-class background and had resented Eleanor's marriage to a clergyman of humble origin.

'The first thing to do is to tuck into Mrs Watkins' shepherd's pie, and then I shall feel fortified to have a word with my father.'

'Perhaps he will come back to Pontywen and work in partnership with you,' I suggested.

'You must be joking. Can you imagine my mother coming back to the smoke and the common people of this town? She hated every minute of their time here in this place. She certainly will not exchange her social life with the hunting and shooting set for incarceration in

Pontywen. My only hope is that Daddy will know some-body somewhere who will be able to help.'

Half an hour later she was on the telephone to her father while I eavesdropped through the open door of my study, pretending to tidy up the chaos of papers on my desk. After ten minutes or so the tone of her voice changed from solicitude to reassurance. 'I'll wait to hear from you then,' she said, and put the phone down. Her face was transformed when she came into the study.

'Thank God for fathers,' I commented.

'Fred, my love, I say "Amen" to that. He said that only this morning he heard from a friend of his that his son was coming out of the Army and was looking for work as a locum. He is going to get in touch with him later today and will let me have the son's address and home number this evening.' She caught hold of me and hugged me so tightly that I thought my rib-cage was going to crack.

'Put me down, you monster,' I commanded. 'You don't know your own strength, a little girl like you. You should be ashamed of yourself.'

'His name is Gareth Andrews, and he trained at Bart's. Daddy said that he met him when he was on leave a few years ago and that he seems an agreeable bloke, as he put it so charmingly. So let's keep our fingers crossed.'

'I should put your hands together as well. I shall certainly do so.'

'By all means, Frederick. I'll stand on my head as well, if necessary.'

What with hands together and fingers crossed, that evening the post in the Pontywen practice was filled. Eleanor phoned Gareth Andrews at his officers' mess in Aldershot and he agreed to the terms she offered him. He was due to be 'demobbed' in a month's time and was looking forward to coming out into the civilian world. He was engaged to be married to a Cardiff girl and until they could find a house in the vicinity he would stay with her parents in Cardiff, travelling up the Valley each day.

To celebrate the occasion, Eleanor and I went out to dinner at the Tudor Arms, where we had had our wedding breakfast-cum-lunch. It was a mock Tudor building erected in the thirties to cater for the elite of the Valleys. This was our first visit there since that milestone in our lives. We were shown to a table for two in an alcove. As we were studying the menu, I heard the loud and unmistakable tones of the rural dean, the Reverend Daniel Thomas, BA, RD. as his notepaper described him.

'Oh, no!' I exclaimed.

'Just keep our heads down and they might not see us,' suggested Eleanor.

'Hello, Vicar!' bellowed the dignitary. 'Fancy seeing you and your good lady! Would you care to join us?'

There was no escape. The waiter showed us to a table for four. Mrs Rural Dean was a fresh-faced, comfortably figured lady with a pleasant smile. Her spouse was a squat little man with a grey, lined face surmounted by a few straggling hairs on his bald head. His beady little eyes were protected by eyebrows which had more hairs than the total of those above.

'Well, well! Fancy meeting you two here. Is it a special occasion or do you come here often?'

I was tempted to say 'Only in the mating season' but I restrained myself.

Eleanor spoke up. 'We have something to celebrate too. I have been without a partner in my very busy practice for the past six months and this evening I have found someone who will be joining me in a month's time.'

'Isn't that good?' said the rural dean to his wife. 'Doctor Seaborne has been doing some very fine work in Pontywen, so I hear – like her husband. Well done, both of you.'

The waiter was hovering behind us. 'Would you care to order some wine?' he asked.

'Let's have some champagne to mark the occasion,' Eleanor suggested.

The rural dean looked at the wine list and his grey face went white.

'Well, we don't drink champagne, only wine. I'm wondering if it will be too strong for driving home afterwards.'

'It's not all that strong,' replied my wife. 'Please allow us to treat you to some. It's not often that we have something like this to celebrate.'

The rural dean's visage returned to its normal grey colour and his beady eyes shone in anticipation of a rare indulgence. 'That's very kind of you, I must say. I think the last time we had champagne was at the wedding of Lord and Lady Llangennith's daughter. She got married in our church in 1935.'

'1936,' corrected his wife with a little smile.

'Was it? I could have sworn it was the year that our sweet peas took first prize at the Abergavenny Flower Show.'

'That was 1937, dear. The same year as the Coronation. Don't you remember our roses came out just in time to decorate the tables in the church hall for the celebration tea? Then, later on, the sweet peas came on in leaps and bounds in time for the show. It was our best year in the garden.'

'I don't know about that. I think 1942 was easily the best. We had that lovely summer after that very cold winter. The flowers may not have been at their best but the vegetables were magnificent. Remember those cauliflowers? One of those would have been enough to feed a family, just on its own, done with some cheese, Doctor Seaton.'

'And do you know why that was the case? The septic tank at the bottom of the garden had overflowed and as the cauliflowers were planted next to it, they had manuring good enough to grow giant plants.'

By this time the wine waiter had arrived with the champagne and the horticultural discussion came to a timely end. Throughout the meal the Reverend Daniel Thomas and his wife continued the duologue, to the quiet amusement of Eleanor and myself. It was a cabaret show *par excellence*.

'Well, thank you both,' said the rural dean as we went into the car park after the meal. 'I hope I shall be able to drive straight after that champagne.'

'It's the corners you've got to watch, Dan, isn't it, Vicar? Any fool can drive straight.'

This remark from Mrs Thomas, delivered with a smile, did not amuse her husband as he struggled with the lock on his car door.

Once inside his precious Morris Oxford which he cherished even more than his garden, he switched on the ignition, to be met with a deathly rattle. After several attempts to start the car while Eleanor and I watched from her new Morris Minor, he dismounted and opened up the bonnet. He stared at the interior in the fading light and then fiddled with the plugs. Back in the car, he tried to arouse the sleeping engine. To no avail.

'Look at your hands, Dan,' said his spouse. 'They are filthy. You'll be having that muck all over your best suit if you're not careful.'

'Never mind my suit, woman,' shouted the dignitary. 'How are we going to get back home?'

'I think the time has come', suggested Eleanor, 'to make ourselves useful.'

'What do you mean?' I asked. 'I don't know one plug from another.'

'Calm down, Frederick. What I am proposing is a tow of their car back to Pentwyn Vicarage. Perhaps the hotel can lend us a rope of some kind. If the rural dean doesn't fancy guiding his car behind ours, you can guide it while I drive.'

'Thank you very much, Eleanor. Let him try a few more times to get the thing started.'

After a few more times the battery surrendered and a deathly silence prevailed.

'You had better come with me to the hotel,' I said to my wife. 'Your female charms will be more effective than my dog collar.'

I went across to the despairing rural dean who was slumped over the wheel of his car, looking into space. 'We are going to see if the hotel can lend us a rope to tow you back home,' I announced.

'Isn't that kind?' said Mrs Thomas. Her husband grunted.

The manager responded to the plaintive appeal of my beloved immediately and produced a tow-rope from a garage at the back of the hotel.

With the help of one of the menials the rope was attached between the two cars.

'Would you like me to guide the car or would you prefer to do it yourself?' I asked the Reverend Daniel Thomas.

'You know what your sight is like, Dan,' said his wife. 'And there is no light coming from your head-lamps. I think you ought to let the vicar take over.'

He offered no objection and moved into the back of the car with Mrs Thomas as if resigned to his fate.

Eleanor switched on the head-lamps of her car with Mrs Thomas as the rural dean's car slithered across the car park.

'You've still got the hand-brake on!' he shouted.

'Sorry, Mr Rural Dean,' I murmured. I fumbled with the brake. By now Eleanor was out of her car and was banging on the window.

'What are you doing?' she demanded.

'I'm afraid I still had the hand-brake on.'

'Then take it off,' she ordered.

'I've done it,' I said.

'Pull the window down. I can't hear you.'

I pulled the window down. 'I've done it, I said.'

'Well, don't shout. We'll move off now and for God's sake keep your eyes on my rear lights! Sorry, Mr Rural Dean,' she added.

As she moved off, I stared as if mesmerized by the lights in front of me. In fairness to Eleanor she drove slowly, but in spite of that, there were bumps in the road where the rural dean's car seemed to disagree with what was happening in front.

Half an hour later Eleanor approached the entrance to Pentwyn Vicarage. It was on a sharp right-hand bend. There was a loud crunch as the car I was steering came in contact with the vicarage gate-post.

'Stop!' I shouted, but the car in front proceeded down the drive. Another clang and the vicarage car broke free of its restraint, making for its home base. As we pulled up outside the haven where it would be, the Reverend Daniel Thomas leaped out of the car with an agility which belied his years.

He dashed into the vicarage porch, frantically putting the key in the front door and then switching on the outside light.

'Look at my car,' he moaned. 'The whole of that door is bashed in. It will never be the same again.'

'I'm sure it will,' said my wife reassuringly. 'Your insurance will cover all the repair to the damage. In a month or so, it will be as good as new.'

'There you are, Dan. The doctor knows. So don't worry!' Mrs Thomas spoke as if there had been a medical check-up.

As we drove away, I said to my wife, 'I don't know what I would do without you.'

'You can say that again,' she replied. 'How else would you escape the consequences of your clerical errors?'

4

'First of all, have you brought with you a card or a sheet of paper with your Christian name printed in big block letters?' The candidates assembled in the nave of St Mary's for the rehearsal of the confirmation looked blankly at me when I asked the question. As each confirmee knelt before the bishop, it had been the custom for the clergymen presenting them to announce the Christian name to the dignitary which he would then repeat before laying his hands upon the head of the candidate. Apparently some of the clergy had not been audible on occasions, causing the bishop embarrassment by having to ask again for the name. There were instances when the candidate was given a name by the bishop which he or she did not possess. In order to avoid further trouble of this nature, we were instructed that the clergyman responsible for the presentation should hold up a card or sheet of paper with the name printed in large capital letters.

Charles Wentworth-Baxter broke the silence with a cough. 'I'm sorry, Vicar,' he mumbled, 'but I'm afraid it slipped my mind to tell them.' I had given him responsibility for the preparation of the thirty candidates who had been in his charge for six months of weekly classes in the church hall. The rehearsal was being held on the Friday before the Sunday evening when the service was due to take place.

'In that case,' I said to them, 'it is just as well that we are having this run through the service tonight. You can cut out a piece of cardboard or a piece of paper about twice the size of a postcard and print the Christian name by which you are known in big thick letters – just the one Christian name.'

One boy put up his hand. 'Please, sir, what if you have a long Christian name but everybody calls you by a short name?'

'That's all right, Monty. Just put Monty, it would take a big piece of card to spell Montgomery. Anyway, everybody calls Field Marshal Montgomery "Monty", don't they?' Monty Jones blushed with pride at being identified with the great war hero.

Another boy raised his hand. It was Llewellyn Waters. 'I'm not shortening my name, Vicar. My mother says that Llewellyn is the name I was given, not Llew which sounds common in any case.' I was beginning to regret my acceptance of the chaplaincy to his father already. The boy's priggish statement was ironic in view of the fact that his father was known throughout Pontywen as Dai Spout.

'Very well, Llewellyn. That's enough about names. Now let's get down to the service. I am going to pretend that I am the bishop, and Mr Wentworth-Baxter will bring each one of you to kneel in front of me on the chancel step where this kneeler is placed. Remember to bow to the bishop before you kneel down. Don't forget to kneel upright. Then when you have been confirmed get up and bow to the bishop once more. Then go back to your pew and say your prayers, thanking God for what he has done for you. By the way, girls, you may curtsey to the bishop if you wish, rather than bow. Boys will come forward first, the boy on the end moving back into the aisle so that the furthest in is the first in each pew to come forward to be confirmed. The same thing with the girls.'

Only Charles could turn this simple procedure into a farce. It began when he proceeded to go to the last row of boys instead of the front row. Having been told to go to the front row, he propelled the boy at the end of the row forward for confirmation, despite a remonstration from the candidate that he was supposed to move back, not forward. 'Jimmy is quite right, Mr Wentworth-Baxter. The boys come out in reverse order, remember.'

'Of course, Vicar, my apologies.' When it came to the rehearsal ritual of confirmation, the curate was so anxious to keep the momentum of candidates coming forward that he was causing the waiting boy to collide with the boy who had just arisen, forgetting that he had to bow to His Lordship before going back to his place.

I decided to avoid any unseemly confusion of this sort on Sunday by announcing that I would shepherd the candidates from the pews and that the curate would present them to the bishop since he was responsible for preparing them for confirmation.

'There's one other thing,' I said when the rehearsal was over. 'I understand that the bishop these days will question you about the catechism. I am sure that Mr Wentworth-Baxter has given you a good grounding in that over the past six months. So don't be afraid to speak up when the time comes.'

Mr Wentworth-Baxter's face dropped at the news. As soon as the candidates had gone, he came up to me. 'I didn't know that the bishop was going to catechize them. If I had been aware of that I would have given them a refresher course over the past few weeks. Is he going to ask questions of them as a group or is he going to pick on one individual?'

'I have no idea, Charles. Anyway, you know His Lordship. If he does ask a question of an individual he will do so kindly, I am positive. I shouldn't lose any sleep over it, if I were you. All you have to do is to hold the cards the right way up and to check that they have brought them with them in the first place. If they haven't, you had better have some material ready for last-minute printing. I suppose you have seen Miss Wright about the veils for the girls.'

Miss Wright was an elderly lady who had been responsible for the confirmation veils for the girls and ladies for many years.

'I'm afraid I haven't, Fred. In any case she will have them ready. She knows the service is on Sunday.'

'That is not the point, Charles. Miss Wright is the kind of person who loves to be visited by the clergy, whether it is just a pastoral call or simply to show interest in what she is doing for the church. Just pop in sometime tomorrow, please.' It was a very disgruntled curate who left the church that evening.

When I told Eleanor about the disgruntlement, she suggested that we should invite Charles and Bronwen to tea with the bishop. It was the custom in Pontywen to have refreshments in the church hall after the service when the bishop would sign the little devotional manuals presented to the candidates. It was also the custom for the vicar to have the company of His Lordship at tea before the service in the evening.

'Perhaps that will appease him. Besides, it will give Bronwen a break from the house. I think her morning sickness has been getting her down, though she would be the last to admit it. She is a tough little girl.'

'She needs to be, my love, with Charles as her husband. If he had a quarter of her quality, I would be happy.'

'Well, Frederick, he hasn't, and it is pointless wishing it were otherwise. Now then, what about you? Have you been to Protheroe the butcher to collect the tongue for his holy highness's sandwiches?'

'Sorry, love. I'll be there first thing tomorrow after Matins, I promise you.'

'I don't know how you have the nerve to persecute your poor downtrodden curate about not doing his duty when you can't carry out promises yourself, you tyrant.'

Next morning I was standing at the back of an impatient queue in the butcher's shop while Jack Protheroe and his wife endeavoured to cope with serving meat and cutting the necessary coupons out of the ration books as quickly as they could. To my dismay I was joined by Agnes Collier who pounced upon me with as much relish as a hungry hawk finding its prey.

'Vicar! Just the man I wanted to see.' She spoke in quiet, confidential tones which boded ill. 'Perhaps we could have a word once we have been served. I can't discuss it here with you in the shop. How is Dr Secombe? I very rarely see her these days now that you are at the vicarage. She must be very busy with this new National Health starting.' Before I could reply to her question about Eleanor's state of health she continued her one-sided conversation. 'Confirmation tomorrow, isn't it? Only seven from St Padarn's. Things are going downhill fast. It was fifteen last time but that was when you were curate. It used to be even more than that before the war. Still, everything was different then. No coupons, no queues.'

By now I was resigned to a half-hour's verbal battering with a possible load of trouble awaiting me once we left the shop. Suddenly deliverance came, the butcher had noticed me at the tail-end of the queue. He produced a parcel of meat from the refrigerator. 'You'd better have this now, Vicar. It will save you waiting.'

There were loud comments from the irate customers. 'It's all right for some.' 'Where's his coupons?'

'Now then, ladies,' shouted Jack Protheroe. 'Fair's fair. The vicar ordered this two days ago and the coupons have been seen to.'

I made my way through the throng and was waylaid by Mrs Collier as I was about to leave the shop. 'What about that talk I wanted with you?' she asked.

'Come and see me at the vicarage on Monday morning.' I thought it wiser to have the encounter on my territory rather than hers.

'In that case, you'll have to give me time to finish my washing, Vicar.'

'Is twelve o'clock convenient for you?'

'I think I can manage it by then. If I can't you'll have to allow me to be a bit late.'

'Not to worry, Mrs Collier.' The later, the better, I said to myself. Then there will be less time to have to listen to whatever she is trying to stir up. For the time being it would be enough to cope with the confirmation service and the visit of the bishop.

Charles had been delighted at the invitation to tea with the bishop. 'It will be a chance for Bronwen to meet His Lordship. Perhaps it will help to change her mind about confirmation.' So far she had been unwilling to take the step. Her allegiance to the Baptist Church had been very strong and her non-attendance at Holy Communion had been the source of much comment at St Padarn's. Her church-going so far had been limited to Evensong.

Sunday morning had dawned warm and sultry. As the

day went on it became hot, and the one o'clock news on the wireless was punctuated by thunder crackles. By the time Mrs Watkins arrived at three o'clock to help with preparation for the tea-party, the sky had turned an inky blue and the first rumbles had began to roll around the hills. 'It do look as if we're in for one of those tropical storms they are forecasting,' she said. 'You should see the lightning further down the valley.'

The next minute there was a blinding flash and a crash of thunder which shook the house. Then the heavens opened and emptied themselves upon Pontywen. For the next half-hour the storm raged, punctuated by fearful forked lightning and a barrage of thunder-claps. A river of water streamed down the vicarage drive.

'It reminds me of Father Whittaker's famous fête,' I said to Eleanor. My predecessor had organized a fête on the vicarage lawn only to be confronted with a similar 'tropical' storm.

'More to the point,' answered my wife, 'it reminds me that one of us had better get down to 13 Mount Pleasant View and bring Charles and Bronwen. A few steps outside the door and they would be soaked to the skin.'

'I'll go. You will need to be here with Mrs Watkins to get the tea ready. The bishop will be here before long, that is, if his car has not been swept off the road by the floods.'

The streets of Pontywen were awash with rainwater as I drove down to the curate's house. Not a soul was to be seen. I pressed on the horn when I arrived. Charles appeared at the front-room window and gave me the thumbs-up sign. A cascade was pouring down the steps when the couple came out huddled under Charles's big umbrella. Inevitably my hapless curate was unable to

57

close the umbrella after Bronwen had been seated in the car.

'Get in, Charles,' I ordered, 'and leave it on the pavement.' Then I made a quick dash from my driving seat, seized it and attempted to close the thing as the rain fell in torrents. I failed to do so. By now exasperated, I told Charles to open his window and hold the extended top as close as possible to the window as he could. I drove off to the vicarage with the umbrella like some large excrescence clinging to the side of the car. We were greeted by Eleanor standing on the doorstep with a look of bewilderment on her face.

'What on earth are you doing, Charles?' she asked. 'The car doesn't need the umbrella. It's meant for you.'

'Let's get in first, then we'll explain,' I said before Charles could answer. He got out holding the umbrella under which Bronwen sheltered. Then I dashed through the downpour to join them.

'Don't close it,' said Eleanor, 'leave it open in the porch for the rain to drain off it.'

'Leaving it open is the easy option,' I replied. 'You try closing it.'

No sooner had we entered the house than the telephone rang. It was the bishop phoning from a call-box. 'I'm afraid I shall be late arriving. There has been severe flooding in the lower part of the valley and the police have advised me to come to you via a circuitous route which will bring me to Pontywen from the top end. Don't worry, Vicar. I am sure I shall be able to make it in time for the service. This deluge can't last much longer.'

'It never rains but it pours,' remarked my wife when I passed on the news.

By six o'clock the storm had passed and the sun shone

once more, but there was no sign of the bishop. We had decided to hold our tea-party without him, leaving him a generous helping of tongue sandwiches and Mrs Watkins' home-made cake for whenever he arrived. The service was due to take place at half past six. So as soon as the rain stopped we made our way across to the church, skirting the pools on the drive.

Already the vestry was full of excited girls who had come to have their veils fixed by Miss Wright. She was involved in an altercation with one of them, Desiree Jones, who was holding a veil, on the verge of tears. 'She wants to wear that thing,' snapped the elderly veil supervisor. 'Show it to the vicar, girl.' Desiree held up the 'thing', a headdress much more suited to a bride than a candidate for confirmation. 'My mother bought it for me specially,' she said, her lower lip quivering. 'Miss Wright says it's to show off but it isn't, Vicar, honest. It's my mother's present for my confirmation.'

'I tell you what, Desiree, we'll ask the bishop when he comes if he minds you wearing it.' Knowing His Lordship, I was certain that by passing the buck to him she would be allowed to wear her mother's present and I would not incur Miss Wright's wrath for granting her permission to be different from the other girls.

A few minutes later a harassed bishop arrived, escorted by David Vaughan-Jenkins, the churchwarden who carried the episcopal case. 'What an afternoon!' exclaimed the dignitary. 'At one time I thought I would be stranded in a patch of water when it seemed to engulf the bottom half of the car. Fortunately the engine kept going and I made it to the outside. The next thing that happened was that I was unable to apply the brakes and had to wait for them to dry out. However, here I am, all in one piece but more than a little weary. I am afraid I shall not be able to stay long after the service, if you will excuse me.'

'Of course, my lord. We are only too pleased that you were able to get here under the circumstances.' As he was about to open his case on the vestry table, I motioned to Desiree to come forward. All the other girls had gone to their places in the nave. 'I wonder if you could spare a moment to look at this young lady's veil, my lord. Her mother bought it as a present for her, not realizing that the veils were supplied by the church. I'm afraid it is rather ornate and very different from those that the rest of the candidates are wearing.'

He turned around, looked at the veil and then looked at Desiree. 'My dear, if it is your mother's present, you wear it.'

Her face was transformed. A smile of delight spread across her features. There was a transformation too in Miss Wright, who was standing by with the standard veil in her hand. She flung it into the open box and stalked out of the vestry.

'Can I put it on myself?' inquired the candidate. 'I have tried it on at home.'

'Of course,' I said. 'Use that mirror in the corner.' A minute later a happy young lady left to join her friends, prepared like a bride adorned for her husband.

'I hope you don't mind, my lord, but I have asked Ezekiel Evans, the lay reader, to act as your chaplain, while I marshal the candidates and Charles Wentworth-Baxter presents them. He has been responsible for the preparation.'

'Not at all, Vicar. I am sure Mr Evans will make an adequate chaplain.'

A tap on my vestry door at that moment heralded the

arrival of the self-important chaplain, bursting with pride at the honour bestowed upon him. 'Hi 'ope, hi ham not h'intruding,' said the face which had appeared around the door. The momentous occasion was producing a plethora of misplaced aspirates.

'Come on in, Mr Evans,' I said. 'The bishop will be glad of your assistance. Perhaps you will excuse me, my lord, while I check that all the candidates have arrived and have settled down in the nave.'

'By all means,' replied His Lordship. 'Mr Evans, I should be pleased if you would help me with my robes.' Ezekiel's cup was overflowing.

I went out to join Charles who was hovering around the chancel steps where the chair had been placed in readiness for the bishop. 'Do you think I have put it too near the edge?' he asked.

'Of course not,' I replied. 'If you put it any further back he would need arms like a gorilla to reach the heads of the candidates. More importantly, have you checked that they have all brought cards with their names on them?'

'Yes, they have all done that except that some of them have used fancy block capitals more appropriate for scrolls than anything else, but I think the bishop will be able to read them.'

As I surveyed the boys with their scrubbed faces and their neatly parted hair I noticed that Llewellyn Waters had plastered his hair with Brylcreem or some such hair oil. 'If His Lordship puts his hands on his head, then on the heads of the girls in their veils, it will take Miss Wright weeks to get the grease out. She is already in high dudgeon. You had better make him the first to be confirmed, Charles, and by the time the bishop has finished with the other boys, most of the grease will have come off on their nice clean hair.'

The son and heir of the future mayor was removed from the back row of the candidates and transferred to the front pew whose occupants had to be removed to accommodate him in the furthermost place. Evidently he thought the move was due to his important status. He stood up and looked around at his mother and father with as much pride as Ezekiel Evans had shown in the vestry. Llewellyn Waters was to be in number one position.

This elevation went to his head in the bishop's address. The first few questions on the catechism had produced silence in the candidates. The bishop tried again. 'What is the outward visible sign or form in baptism?' Llewellyn's hand shot up. 'Yes?' inquired His Lordship. 'The baby,' said Llewellyn triumphantly. An unseemly burst of laughter erupted from the congregation to the great embarrassment of Councillor and Mrs Waters whose heads were bent as if in prayer that they should be swallowed up and removed from the nave of St Mary's Church, Pontywen.

After that response from the candidate, the bishop abandoned any further attempts to catechize and suggested that it might be well if the newly confirmed continued to go to classes for another six months, when they might learn something to their advantage. Charles tried to hide himself in his stall by turning his back to the congregation and burying his face in a prayer-book.

When the bishop had finished his address and the second hymn had begun, Ezekiel Evans stepped forward to begin his chaplaincy duties. In so doing he engaged in a *pas de deux* with the curate who had vacated his stall to begin his presentation duty. After they had sorted themselves out Ezekiel was handed a large card by the bishop on which the service was printed in large letters. This had to be held in front of him by the chaplain. In the meanwhile Charles had taken up his place on the right hand of His Lordship, ready to present his under-prepared charges.

First the bishop asked the candidates to stand, then motioned to Ezekiel Evans to hold up the service card. The lay reader must have been under the impression that the prelate was shortsighted. He made an elaborate bow and advanced upon His Lordship with the apparent intent of rubbing his nose in the print. After his sight line had been adjusted the bishop read the opening prayer and then asked the confirmed if they would renew the promises made at their baptism. Instead of the loud response we had practised at the rehearsal, he received a barely audible 'I do'. One more prayer and the moment of the laying-on of hands had arrived.

I went down to the front pew to organize the shepherding of the candidates. The five boys moved out in order to allow Llewellyn Waters to be the first to kneel in front of the bishop. Ezekiel's bow paled into insignificance compared with that of the councillor's son who then forgot to hand Charles his card with his printed name. As the boy was in the process of kneeling, the curate darted forward and seized the card which he held up for scrutiny.

The Bishop stared at it uncomprehendingly. 'His name,' he snapped uncharacteristically.

'Er, Llewellyn,' said the curate nervously, looking at the card he had held up and realizing too late that it was upside-down.

Apart from some fumbling of the cards, the rest of the

candidates were confirmed without any hitch. When the service was over the bishop took Charles aside in the vestry and gave him a gentle lecture. 'I know it is not easy to prepare these young people nowadays, what with the wireless and the cinema and all the other distractions to take their minds off more serious matters, but it is your duty to see that they are ready for confirmation. They should know their catechism and not only know it but understand it. If I were you, I should see to it that they meet for a few months at least to receive further instruction. Some bishops might have refused to confirm the candidates if they had had the response your young people gave me.'

It was a very tired dignitary who sat down in the church hall to consume the tongue sandwiches and the homemade cake. 'This has been a long day, Vicar, and if you don't mind, once I have signed the manuals I must go.'

When the bishop had satisfied his hunger he came out from the side room in which he had been closeted and was confronted with the hubbub of the crowded hall, a scrum of the newly confirmed fighting to be first in the queue to have their little books signed. Despite his fatigue, he had a word with each of the confirmed while their parents looked on with pride at their offspring.

One of the last to produce his manual for signing was Llewellyn Waters, watched by his father and mother who had now recovered their composure. As the Bishop handed the boy his signed copy, Dai Spout announced that he was to be mayor next month and that the vicar was to be his chaplain.

'I hope you have a happy term of office, councillor,' said the bishop. 'You have a very competent chaplain, I can assure you.'

As the bishop left, the mayor-elect said to me, 'What a nice man! You could see that he understood what Llewellyn meant when he said that the baby was the visible part of baptism. That is a logical statement after all, as it were.'

5

'What a fiasco!' said my curate. 'Those stupid kids, sitting like mummies, apart, of course, from Dai Spout junior whose intelligence is minimal but whose mouth is as big as his father's. It would have been far better if he had kept it shut, like the rest.'

'If you don't mind me saying so,' I replied, 'you really have a nerve to talk about a fiasco. Whose fault was that? Had those "kids", as you call them, been adequately instructed in the catechism, all would have been well. As for Llewellyn Waters and his father, don't forget that I shall have to spend many hours in Councillor Waters' company during the next twelve months. It doesn't help to hear you taking him apart like that. There is something to be said for young Waters. At least he did speak up. Anyway, as a result of the fiasco you will have to keep to the bishop's instruction and hold classes for the newly confirmed over the next six months or so.'

'Fred! You don't mean that. Bronwen is going to need me very much over these next six months. I didn't think it was an instruction from His Lordship. It was more in the nature of a suggestion.'

'Charles, you may have considered it as a suggestion but as far as I am concerned it is an instruction. Half an hour a week is hardly going to take you away from your wife's side a great amount. I hope you don't think that Bronwen's pregnancy gives you *carte blanche* to evade your duties. I'm sure she will not expect you to do so.

Perhaps next time you are supposed to prepare candidates for confirmation you will give them the thorough grounding to which they are entitled.'

So ended the post mortem on the previous evening's events. As we drank our coffee in my study Charles maintained a sulky silence until his departure. An hour later a ring on the doorbell announced the arrival of Mrs Agnes Collier, still flushed with the exertions of her Monday morning laundry, coupled with her brisk walk to the vicarage, indicated by her breathlessness.

'Come on in, Mrs Collier,' I said with a show of feigned bonhomie. She simulated a smile and stalked into the study. As she seated herself in the armchair she gave the impression that like Eliza she had come to stay.

'Now, what can I do for you?' I asked.

'I don't know how to put this, Vicar. It's a very delicate matter but I thought you should know about it before it becomes serious – that is, if it isn't already, if you know what I mean.'

'Well, Mrs Collier, since you haven't told me anything so far, how can I know what you mean?'

Agnes leaned forward confidentially. 'It's – er – about the organist and one of the choir-boys.' She stopped speaking and looked at me to see if I was shocked.

'What about the organist and the choir-boy?' My matter-of-fact tone of voice disconcerted her. She fiddled with her handbag.

'I suppose I had better begin at the beginning, Vicar. I know he's a good organist. Not as good as my late husband, of course, but he does know how to play the organ. I'll give him that. Still, that's beside the point.' She paused for breath.

'Before you go any further, Mrs Collier,' I interrupted.

'I have heard the allegation about Albert Williams and young David Morris which you passed on to other people who passed them on to me. Unless you have something specific to say about the relationship, I would advise you to keep quiet on the subject. Otherwise you may find yourself the subject of a slander action which would be bad for you and for St Padarn's.'

Her eyes had the glazed look of a boxer who had been caught with a knockout punch. She sat silent and stared into space. Then she stood up abruptly and turned her gaze on me. It was a remarkable transformation. Now her face was red with indignation, her eyes burning into mine.

'It isn't a slander case against me you've got to worry about, Vicar. It will be a very nasty case against Albert Williams. I've seen the way he looks at young David and if it comes to that, the way the boy looks at him. There's something going on there, believe me, and if you are going to shut your eyes to it, you'll have to take the consequences. As far as St Padarn's is concerned, the last thing we want is a scandal, it's bad enough now with Mr Wentworth-Baxter in charge. The congregation is going down every Sunday. Get a scandal and the place will be empty. Well, you can't say I haven't warned you. Good morning, Vicar!' So saying, she picked up her handbag from the chair and made an exit worthy of Dame Sybil Thorndike at her magisterial best.

'I wish to heaven I had never appointed Albert Williams as organist,' I said to Eleanor when she came in from her rounds. 'It has meant nothing but trouble ever since he started. As old Canon Llewellyn used to say, wherever there is a choir there is the devil.'

'In that case, Frederick,' she replied, 'perhaps you had better do some exorcism and remove the devil.'

'If I get rid of Albert, it looks as if I am being ruled by Agnes Collier and Co., and I have no desire to give that impression.'

'Well, my love. Sooner or later you will have to do something, it would seem.'

As it turned out, it was sooner rather than later, that very afternoon. As I was about to leave the vicarage to do some hospital visiting, I had a phone call from Evan Jones, the churchwarden at Llanhyfryd. Evan had a large farm on the outskirts of the parish. He had been a troublemaker when I first came to Pontywen as a curate, but ever since his wife had been treated successfully by Eleanor for a long-standing complaint in her legs, he had ceased to be a thorn in my flesh. His affliction was a painful stammer from which he had suffered since childhood.

'V-Vicar, c-could you c-come round s-sometime t-today? I c-can't talk about it on the ph-phone. It is a b-bit p-personal, like.'

'By all means, Mr Jones. I have to visit the hospital first and then I'll come and see you afterwards.'

'Th-thank you, Vicar. I think you sh-should know about it straight away.'

There were only three patients I had to see at the hospital: one, an elderly lady who loved a gossip, was asleep, whilst the other two patients were less inclined to detain me. As a result, after half an hour I was on my way to Blaenycwm Farm, wondering what the church-warden's mysterious call signified.

It was a lovely afternoon, and once I was out of the smoke which affected Pontywen the sun shone gloriously over the patterned hills of Llanhyfryd. I dawdled my way, feasting on the scenery through the open window of my old Morris Minor and forgetting for the moment the purpose of my visit to Evan Jones. All too soon I had to turn off the main road and crawl up the cart-track that led to Blaenycwm. As I pulled up outside the farmhouse, Del, the black and white sheepdog, announced my presence with a series of barks. On my first visit to the farm he had bitten me on the leg. Since that painful meeting for both of us, when I had retaliated with a kick in his ribs, he had treated me circumspectly. As I got out of the car, he recognized me and kept his distance, content just to glance at me.

Before I could knock on the door the old churchwarden opened it and invited me in with an expansive gesture. 'You d-don't mind coming through to the k-kitchen, Vicar? Mrs Jones is having her af-afternoon n-nap in the f-front room – that's if D-del hasn't w-woken her up.' He pulled out a kitchen chair by the long scrubbed table. 'S-sit yourself down. W-would you l-like a g-glass of cider?' Evan Jones's scrumpy was very potent.

'Just one glass, Mr Jones. I want to drive home straight.'

'R-right you are, Vicar.' He went to the cupboard and produced a large tankard which he proceeded to fill from a stone jar. 'I w-won't join you, if you don't m-mind. I had m-mine with my m-meal earlier on.'

He sat down beside me. 'I w-was going to ring on S-Saturday night but then I thought it b-better to g-get the S-Sunday out of the w-way first. It's a v-very delicate m-matter and I th-thought you should know about it as soon as p-possible.'

It was plain that he was very embarrassed about what he had to say. 'Well, l-last Saturday afternoon, I w-went d-down to the h-hay field to s-see if it w-was ready for

c-cutting. W-When I opened the g-gate I found two b-bicycles l-lying against the h-hedge. Then I n-noticed that s-somebody had b-been walking into the field. A c-couple I thought trampling d-down my hay. S-so I followed the t-track they had made and sh-shouted, "C-come out of there" – b-but it wasn't a c-couple. It was a m-man and a b-boy. They were d-doing up their t-trousers. "Get out of here b-before I c-call the p-police," I said. They were out l-like a shot on their b-bikes and d-down that lane like b-bats out of hell. The t-trouble is, Vicar, I think the man was the one who is the or-organist you've p-put in St Padarn's, the one with the g-glasses who used to h-help in the p-parish church. I m-may be wrong b-but I'm willing to b-bet it was him.'

'Thank you, Mr Jones, for telling me this. Have you mentioned it to anybody else?'

'N-no. It's n-not the kind of thing you t-talk about. I

's-suppose the p-police should know. Anyway I l-leave it to you. You know b-best. S-something will have to be d-done about it, th-that's for sure.'

'Let me think this over. Whatever is done, will have to be done for the best. There's the boy's future to be considered. If the case comes to the courts, he will have to give evidence and he will be the centre of gossip as much as the man. I shall let you know what happens and in the meantime I would be obliged if you say nothing to anybody.'

'I'll d-do that, Vicar. I h-haven't even told my wife. Now then, Vicar, c-come on, drink up that cider. I'll g-go and see if my w-wife is awake. I expect she'll like to s-see you before you l-leave.'

As he went down the corridor, I took a deep drink of the ice-cool cider and wondered why on earth I had wanted to become a vicar so soon. If I were still a curate I could pass on the responsibility for action to my boss whose years of experience as a pastor would make him better qualified to deal with this messy situation.

The sun still shone gloriously as I drove back to Pontywen, but it failed to penetrate the gloom which had enveloped me. David Morris was a good-looking twelve-year-old. Tall for his age, he had blond curly hair and vividly blue eyes. An intelligent child, he had passed his eleven-plus and was doing well in Pontywen Grammar School. An only child, he was adored by his parents who kept a newspaper and confectionery shop on the council housing estate. His father, Glyn Morris, was a burly man, notoriously short-tempered. If he found out that his son had been seduced, Albert Williams would go in danger of his life. It was a prospect which sent shivers down my spine.

When I arrived back at the vicarage, Eleanor had not yet left for her early evening surgery. She looked at my face as I entered the kitchen. 'You're as pale as a ghost,' she commented. 'What has old Jones told you?'

'Can you spare a few minutes?' I asked.

'By all means,' she replied. 'Longer if you like. It's obvious that you have had a shock. Let's sit down in the lounge.'

She sat beside me on the settee and held my hand.

'Well, I can hardly describe it as a shock since it was something I had expected.'

'Don't tell me, love. It's Albert Williams, isn't it?'

'Right, first time. Last Saturday afternoon, Evan went down to inspect his hayfield to decide whether it was ready for harvest and he found Albert Williams and young David either after the act or just before the act – anyway, they were "doing up their trousers", as he put it. He threatened to call the police and they were off down the lane as fast as their bikes could take them. He has not told anybody about it, not even his wife. He thought the police should know about it but has left it to me to decide what to do. As far as I am concerned, the last thing I want to happen is to have the police involved. That would give Pontywen something to gossip about for the next twelve months, apart from the effect on young David and his family.'

'Well, as far as the police are concerned, there is no evidence to convict Albert Williams. They were not caught "*in flagrante delicto*". So that doesn't arise. On the other hand Albert Williams must go from St Padarn's immediately.'

'I know that, love. What worries me is whether I should have a word with David or not. He is a very sensitive child and if he knows that I am aware that he has been involved in something which is an offence he will have a guilt complex which could cripple him psychologically, possibly for the rest of his life. Whatever happens, his parents mustn't know what has happened. His father would throttle Albert.'

'That's something we can talk about later tonight. In some ways, I'm glad this has happened. It means that you will be able to remove the seat of the trouble – Albert Williams. If a surgical operation can remove the cause of the cancer, that is sometimes all that matters. Everything else is of secondary importance.'

As soon as we had finished dinner that evening I said to Eleanor, 'If you don't mind, we can leave our discussion about David Morris till later. I feel I have to remove the cancer, as you put it, forthwith. I hope Albert is in, I don't want to leave it until tomorrow, if I can possibly help it. My cup of anger is running over at the moment. The hotter I can make it for that young man the better.'

'Go to it, Secombe,' replied my wife. 'Frighten the life out of him.'

With my foot firmly on the accelerator I shot through the streets of Pontywen and pulled up outside the Williamses' house with a screech of tyres worthy of a police car in a raid. As I walked up the path, I could hear the piano being played. He was in. My heart beat faster as I contemplated the tirade I intended to inflict upon him. I pressed hard upon the button of the doorbell. There was no response from inside. The piano music continued. I pressed harder this time, the music stopped abruptly. A door was opened and closed with a bang as if Albert was annoyed at the interruption. He flung open the front door. The frown vanished from his face when he saw me, to be replaced by a look of apprehension as he contemplated my angry visage.

'Sorry to keep you waiting, Vicar. I'm afraid I was engrossed by my music. My mother is out at my aunt's. Please come in.' He led me into the front room. 'Take a seat, Vicar.' He pointed to an armchair.

'I won't sit down if you don't mind, Albert. What I have to say is best said standing.' His rosy complexion flushed into a purple. 'Where were you last Saturday afternoon and who was your companion?'

He began to bluster. 'What's all this about, Vicar? What I do outside the church is nothing to do with you.'

'On the contrary,' I shouted, 'it has a great deal to do with me when it concerns any of the choir-boys from my parish, especially when you are discovered in an extremely compromising situation, lying down hidden away in a hay-field.'

'What do you mean by compromising situation? David and I were just out for a ride on our bicycles and as it was such a lovely afternoon, we rested in a field.'

'Come off it, Albert. The farmer discovered you and the boy doing up your trousers hidden away amongst the hay. You are very lucky that he did not contact the police. Otherwise you would have been having a visit from PC Davies instead of me, with a holiday in Cardiff Jail to follow. I warned you not to have any contact with that boy, except in the context of choir practice. This is the end of your connection with St Padarn's. Under no circumstances will you have anything more to do with the organ and certainly not with the choir-boys. Think of the effect you have had on young David and what his parents would do if they knew.'

He collapsed into an armchair and began to weep. 'I

love that boy. He is a delightful boy, in his way I think he loves me. I didn't want to corrupt him. What happened last Saturday afternoon was just a natural expression of our love for each other. It was the first time, I promise you. Now I know that it's the last time.' His sobs became uncontrollable. I waited until they had died down. He pulled out his handkerchief, wiped his eyes and blew his nose. Suddenly I felt sorry for him. It was obvious that his homosexuality was going to bedevil him for the rest of his life.

I sat down in the armchair opposite him. 'Look, Albert. I realize that your sexual inclinations draw you to those of the same sex as yourself. If you indulge them you are going to come into conflict with the law of the land. For your own sake and especially for the sake of those to whom you are attracted, like young David Morris, you must learn to sublimate these feelings in some way or another. You have outstanding musical gifts. Pour your heart into them. Let them suck up your emotions. Don't go looking for another David. That's the road to ruin. I think I had better go now. I'll see myself out. You had better compose yourself before your mother comes back.'

He sat with his head bowed as I left the room and made my way down the garden path to my car. As I drove, I wondered what reason he would give to his mother for his departure from St Padarn's and what reason I would give to the congregation. There would be one person who would guess why he had gone and who would rejoice at his going. Agnes Collier would be convinced that her warning to me was responsible for it.

When I gave Eleanor the account of what had happened she said, 'I feel sorry for him, trapped inside his own nature. I expect he will shed more tears tonight in the privacy of his bedroom. I wonder if David will do the same when he discovers that the affair has ended or whether he will have forgotten all about it in no time, and no tears shed.'

'Which brings me to what I should do about the boy. If he will have forgotten about it as quickly as that then there will be no point in me saying anything to him. However, if this relationship has become a deep one, then I think I owe it to him to have a talk about it. David is a very sensitive lad. I should imagine that the experience is not one which he will shrug off easily.'

'You know him better than I, love. If that is your impression, by all means have a talk with him. He will not be able to turn to his parents for help and guidance, that's certain.'

'It's going to be a much tougher assignment than tearing a strip off Albert Williams. I can't go and see him at his house for obvious reasons. It will be awkward to get any privacy in the vestry. The best plan, I think, will be to meet him outside school tomorrow afternoon and have a word with him in the car.'

The following afternoon I parked the car near the gates of Pontywen Grammar School and waited for the eruption of pupils when school-time had ended. Promptly at four o'clock the exodus began with some of the sixth formers strolling through the yard, followed a few minutes later by a rush of first and second formers, some of them swinging their satchels in combat with each other. Bringing up the rear, in school cap and blazer and with his satchel slung over his back, was David Morris.

I alighted from the car and met him as he was coming through the gates. 'David,' I said. 'Just the boy I want to see.' He looked at me quizzically. 'I should like to have a little talk with you, if I may. My car is just across the road.'

As he sat in the front seat alongside me, I felt angry again that this likable and innocent boy had been led into such a situation. I fumbled in my mind to find a suitable way to broach the subject. It would have been easier if I could have indulged in trivial remarks to lead up to it but my anger with Albert Williams made such an approach impossible. We sat in silence for a short time while the boy's bewilderment gave way to a mixture of embarrassment and trepidation.

'I don't know how to put this, David, but I must tell you that I know about your relationship with Albert Williams, and especially about the incident in a hayfield last Saturday afternoon.'

His face lost all its colour. 'You're not going to tell my parents, are you, sir? My father would kill me if he knew. I told them I was going out for a ride with my friend down the road.'

'Is that the first and only time that you have done that with him?'

'Yes, sir. I swear it is. It won't happen again, sir, honest.'

'You realize that you broke the law when you did it and that Albert Williams could go to prison if it was reported to the police? Mr Evan Jones, the farmer, told me that he had thought of telling PC Davies but, instead, he came to me with the story. You have been a very lucky boy, David, that it hasn't gone any further.'

'I'm sorry, sir, very sorry. Perhaps I should give up the choir to keep away from Albert.'

'You won't have to do that. I have been to see him and told him that he has got to leave St Padarn's and that he must not have anything more to do with you.'

'Thank you, sir. Can I go now? My parents will be wondering why I'm late coming home.'

'I'll drive you as far as Inkerman Street and you can walk from there. You won't be all that late then.'

As we drove off, he said, 'Thank you, Vicar, for not telling my mother and father, I promise I won't ever do anything like that again. I knew it was wrong when he did it to me but he said it wasn't wrong because he loved me and it was his way of showing it.'

I pulled up on the corner of Inkerman Street. 'There's my friend, sir,' he said. 'I'll catch him up. He won't half be jealous when I tell him I've had a ride in your car.'

'So much for my worry that David Morris would be deeply affected by his experience with Albert Williams,' I said to Eleanor later that evening. 'He was much more concerned that I would tell his parents than anything else. It is obvious that Albert's claim that the boy reciprocated his affection was a self-manufactured delusion. There were no tears from David – just relief that the whole episode was over.'

'Thank God for that. I am afraid it is going to be vastly different for Albert – it is all very well you telling him to sublimate his feelings by burying himself in his music. For one thing, you have taken him away from the organ and the choir. Secondly, if he still had that outlet, it would not prevent him from giving way to his inclinations.'

'Well, that is what we were taught in the theological college in a lecture on how to deal with homosexuals. Sympathy for their plight and sublimation as the remedy for their condition.'

'What superficial bilge! His inclinations, as you call them, will never go away. It may be that Albert will try to sublimate them with an overdose of tablets now that he has been found out. I would have thought that a better idea would be for him to get a transfer from the bank in Pontywen to a big city. He could settle down away from his mother and make his friendships with men of his own age where his inclinations would not be noticed as they are in a small town like Pontywen.'

'But that would be condoning a grave sin, if I advised him to do that.'

'For God's sake, Fred, why don't you grow up?' she exploded. 'All you have done with your so-called advice is push him deeper into the mire.'

'I resent that. I did what I thought was right. I can't do any more than that.'

'Sometimes you are pathetic. If you don't mind, I'm going to bed. I've got a busy day ahead of me tomorrow. Goodnight.' She closed the door with a bang.

It was our first real quarrel. I stayed downstairs and listened to the wireless until they played the National Anthem to end the programme for the day. I spent a restless night on the edge of the bed, manufacturing arguments to justify myself which I could use in the morning.

When the alarm clock went off, I was in a deep sleep, exhausted by my mental effort. I put my hand out and turned it off. The next thing I knew I was being kissed on the cheek by my wife, who was in her dressing-gown. 'Wake up, sleeping beauty. There's a cup of tea on the bedside cabinet. I'm off for my bath.'

I never used the arguments, being only too happy that yesterday had gone and that today was a new day with peace restored. It was some weeks later that they told me at the bank that Albert had been transferred to a branch in West London.

6

'We've reserved a seat for you, Dr Secombe, in the front row of the gallery. You'll have a beautiful view of all the proceedings from up by there. Our Llewellyn will be sitting next to you, so you'll have company. I've told him he's got to behave himself. So he won't be any trouble to you.'

Blodwen Waters had pinned us in a corner of the mayor's parlour prior to the mayor-making ceremony. The first time I had met her was when she was in a bed in Pontywen Hospital. It was my initial sick visit in the parish as a raw beginner. I had learnt two important lessons from that encounter – never to ask a female patient what was wrong with her and never to ask to say prayers with someone who rarely attends church. The first question elicited a blush and the single word 'internal', and the second a panicky 'No, thank you. Have they told you something I don't know?'

On that occasion some three years previously Blodwen's hair was dyed a colour which was a messy compromise between pink and red with dark roots in attendance. Today she displayed a glorious, unadulterated scarlet head, evidently intended to match the colour of her mayoral robes. With her beaky nose and pointed chin, she would look like a bird of paradise later that afternoon.

The Mayor's Parlour was as dingy as the rest of Abergwynlais Town Hall. The building was a red-brick monstrosity erected in the early years of the century when industry flourished in the Valley. It was a monument to coal, steel, sweated labour and bad taste. The neglect of the thirties and the war years combined to give it the appearance of a municipal slum, with its peeling paint and accumulation of grime. Three potted palm plants which appeared to be languishing for the sun were the only adornments in the room, apart from an enlarged photograph of the Prince of Wales (in his bowler hat and long coat) visiting the Valleys in the depression of the thirties when he uttered the famous remark, 'Something must be done.'

Councillor David Waters was engaged in earnest conversation with the outgoing mayor, Councillor David Thomas, who was clad in his roles of office for the last time. The mayoress, Mrs Rhoda Thomas, a large, comfortably padded lady, was similarly clad and enjoying a joke with the mayor's secretary, Mr Frank James, a little bespectacled man in a black pin-striped suit, as much a badge of office as the mayoral robes.

Just as Eleanor was beginning to wilt under the endless stream of trivialities pouring forth from Blodwen Waters, Frank James came to her rescue and suggested that the time had come to escort her and Llewellyn to their places in the gallery. The Mayor's Parlour led directly into the Council Chamber and as the secretary opened the door a loud hubbub of conversation emerged. To my great relief Blodwen transferred her attention to Rhoda.

'I'm going to get swamped in that robe, Rhoda, and as for that hat it's going to be murder for my hair. They spent hours in the hairdresser's yesterday doing me up.'

'I can see that,' said her counterpart drily. 'You'll soon get used to wearing it. You can use hairpins to clip it to your head, if you want to. That's what I do, anyway.'

'Come over here, Vicar, and join us,' said David Thomas. 'You don't want to get caught up with women's talk over by there. They've laid on a nice reception for us in the banqueting 'all, you'll be pleased to know. Dai here has seen to that, 'aven't you, Dai?'

'Well, let's put it this way, as it were. Within the limits of these frugal times, as it were, there's quite a good little spread waiting, sit-down, not standing-up buffet. I thought it would give a fine kick-off to my year of office.'

'I like that phrase "frugal times", Dai. It makes a change from "austerity". That word has just about been done to death. I should use "frugal times" in some of your speeches. Well, "frugal times" or not, Vicar. I am sure you will enjoy being Mayor's Chaplain. I know my little man did, Minister of Aberdulais Cong, Elfed Rees Williams. Have you met him?'

'No, Mr Mayor. I'm afraid I haven't. Is he here today?'

'Had to take a funeral of one of the deacons. Business before pleasure, that's it, isn't it, Vicar?'

At this stage in the conversation Frank James re-entered with a request that we get ready to proceed into the Chamber. 'You go first, Mr Chaplain. Stand by the chair far right, Councillor and Mrs Waters to the chairs on either side of the mayor and mayoress. Are you all ready?' Mrs Waters patted her hair and took a deep breath.

The mayor's secretary flung open the door and shouted, 'Will you all be upstanding, please, for your mayor and mayoress, the mayor-elect and the mayoress-elect and their chaplain.' For a little man he had a tremendous voice, one which any boxing MC would envy. 'Right, off you go, Vicar,' he whispered.

I moved forward and tripped as I caught my foot in the

bottom of my cassock, a favourite trick of mine. I saved
myself from falling headlong by grabbing the curtain
which was used to exclude the draught. Unfortunately
the force I applied to the grab was sufficient to pull down
the pole to which it was attached. The chaplain-elect, the
mayor-elect and the mayoress-elect were enveloped in the
musty folds, to the great amusement of the incumbent
mayor and mayoress and to those in the Chamber who
could see the incident. By the time we had disentangled
ourselves, Blodwen Waters' face was as scarlet as her
disarranged hair.

'What a bloody start!' she exclaimed. 'Sorry, Vicar, but
look at my hair. It looks as if I've been pulled through an
'edge backwards. I'll 'ave to comb it before I can go in
there. Excuse me.' She disappeared and went into the toilet
which was in the corridor outside the Mayor's Parlour.

In the meanwhile the occupants of the Council

Chamber were still on their feet. Frank James went back out and shouted, 'Will you all take your seats for a minute or two?' 'Another cover-up is it?' shouted a wag. The mayor's secretary closed the door. I pulled up my cassock and adjusted my belt.

'It's a pity you hadn't done that earlier,' said the mayor-elect. 'Then we wouldn't have had all this mess.'

'Don't shoot the pianist,' interjected the mayor. 'He's doing his best. In any case, you'll have to watch yourself, Dai. It's very easy to trip over these robes, believe me. That's right, isn't it, Rhoda?'

'Oh yes, it is. I've tripped over a few times this last year. Your Blodwen will have to watch it because she's a lot thinner and smaller than me. Perhaps it's a good thing it's happened now. So that you can watch out yourselves every time you dress up.'

How I wished I had been their chaplain.

It must have been at least ten minutes before Blodwen returned, her hair once more immaculate but with a face like thunder.

'I was telling Dai that you will have to watch your robes, Blodwen, in case you trip over them. It's easily done,' said the mayoress.

'I can look after them very well, Rhoda, thank you. Once bitten, twice shy.'

'Well done, Blodwen, but remember the other proverb, pride goes before a fall.' The mayor received one of Blodwen's special dagger-looks for this remark.

'Now, then. Shall we line up again?' requested the mayor's secretary. 'The same order as before. I'll put the curtain back up while you're in the Chamber.'

Once again he opened the door and shouted his announcement.

This time with my cassock tucked up so far that I had a large bulge above the belt and a large expanse of trousers visible, I led the procession on to the platform. When I reached my chair at the far end and turned to face the assembly, I looked up to see my beloved in the front row of the gallery with a large grin upon her countenance as if she were enjoying some hilarious pantomime. Most of the audience seemed to be sharing the same amusement.

When the mayoral entourage was in position, the mayor in his capacity as chairman asked the councillors and the guests to be seated. Below us on the right hand side was the town clerk, bewigged and gowned. Unlike the mayor's secretary, Daniel Harries-Jones was a tall, broad-shouldered individual, a tyrant to his underlings. He had been described to me once by the Vicar of Abergwynlais as a balloon of pomposity. 'Why a balloon?' I had asked. 'According to the dictionary a balloon is anything which is hollow and inflated,' was the reply.

'Before I ask the town clerk to swear in my successor,' said the mayor, 'I must say my few words and I promise you they will be few. I've always used this recipe for public speaking: "Stand up, speak up and shut up."'' As he made this remark he turned to Dai Spout at his side who may have known how to speak up but who certainly never knew how to shut up. The observation was not lost on his listeners.

'I have enjoyed my year of office tremendously. It is good to see how we are settling down in the Valley after the last war. There are problems, for example we have got to build more council houses for the men who have done their bit in the Forces and indeed those who have worked so hard at the coal-face. I know all about that, being a miner myself. We've made a start these last twelve months and I'm sure the new mayor will do all he can to build on it.

'David Waters has served this council for many years faithfully and is now the senior councillor. He has earned the right to this office and I am sure he will be worthy of it. I extend my best wishes to him and his good lady and hope he will enjoy his year as mayor as much as I have done.'

Then he called on the town clerk to administer the swearing-in ceremony. Daniel Harries-Jones made a great show of standing up and smoothing down his gown. He mounted the platform and handed the councillor a bible. Holding it with a shaking hand, the mayor-elect promised that he would be an impartial chairman and a faithful servant of the community. After this he signed the document on a small desk at the side of the platform.

As the audience applauded the mayoral chain of office and the mayoral robes were placed on the new mayor by his predecessor and likewise on the new mayoress by her predecessor. Once enveloped in his scarlet robes, the Mayor of Abergwynlais stepped forward to deliver his mayoral address.

'Thank you, Councillor Thomas, for your kind words, much appreciated. Well, here we are gathered together on this auspicious occasion, representing, as it were, the hopes and aspirations of the borough of Abergwynlais. There's so much to say. I have not written a speech. I speak from the heart, as it were, not from a piece of paper.'

The next quarter of an hour dragged by as the audience must have wished he had confined himself to a piece of paper – many heads were nodding by the time he had finished his peroration. Then he turned to me and announced, 'I have appointed as my chaplain the Reverend Frederick Secombe, Vicar of Pontywen, and I will now ask him to say a few prayers.'

To say that this request was a great shock to me would be an understatement. I had not been given any advance notice that I was to lead the council members and guests in prayer. Furthermore, I was not trained in the art of extempore prayer. Unlike the new mayor, I needed 'a piece of paper' to read if I was to pray publicly. 'Will you all please stand?' I found myself saying, my mouth dry, my tongue cleaving to my gums. There was a long pause. 'Shall we say together the Lord's Prayer?' While my mouth was repeating the familiar words, my mind was racing frantically to find something to say afterwards. By the time the 'Amen' had arrived there was still a void waiting to be filled. A much longer pause ensued. Beads of sweat anointed my forehead. My heart was pumping fast.

Suddenly there came into my head the opening words of the marriage psalm, 'God be merciful unto us and bless us'. Then I added, 'Especially us in the borough of Abergwynlais and thy servant David. Show him the light of thy countenance and be merciful unto him during his year of office through Jesus Christ Our Lord.' There followed the blessing from the communion service, which I knew by heart, and the 'prayers' were over.

Back in the Mayor's Parlour, David Thomas said to me, 'You are going to be a great asset and example to the mayor, short and straight to the point. I liked "thy servant David". It sounded very biblical. My chap never said that.'

In no time, the room was full of councillors and guests.

Eleanor cornered me. 'Trust you to put on a show. What should have been "ring up the curtain" became "ring down" the curtain before anything had started. By the way, there was a mistake in your few words to the Almighty. You should have said, "Be merciful to us during his year of office".'

The new mayor and mayoress were receiving congratulations from all and sundry while their offspring was raiding a plate of biscuits he had discovered on a side table. Eleanor and I were now trapped by the town clerk who was delivering a monologue on the importance of his office. Relief came when the mayor banged the desk with an empty ink pot.

'I'm pleased to tell you that for the first time since the war there is a sit-down meal awaiting you in the banqueting hall. You will find your names at your places and there is a table plan by the door as you come in. There will be glasses of sherry served to you down there and there will be wine with the meal. For this piece of resistance, as it were, in these frugal times I am grateful to an anonymous donor.'

'Anonymous. Bloody funny,' said a voice behind us. 'That's Evans and Watkins. They've just been given the contract to build the new school in Llandenis. I shouldn't be surprised if that isn't all that they have been given.'

I turned around to see Councillor Bill Owen, the only Communist member of the council, known locally as Bill Moscow, a little man whose face was decorated with a few blue scars, the miner's trademark.

'If I were you,' warned the town clerk, 'I should keep comments like that to yourself. Otherwise you could find yourself in trouble, Councillor Owen.'

Bill Owen winked at me and then looked up at the

figure towering above him. 'A Daniel come to judgment, is it?' Daniel Harries-Jones glared at the ex-miner. 'I tell you what, Mr Town Clerk, don't you threaten me, I've eaten bigger men than you for breakfast.' Faced by this challenge, the chief municipal officer moved away quickly to join the throng who were pressing towards the exit like the excited crowds in Cardiff Arms Park after a Welsh victory and anticipating a drink to celebrate.

'Look at them, Vicar,' said Bill Owen. 'As Karl Marx said, "A man is what he eats", and that just about describes them, or as your lot describes them in the Bible, like the Gadarene swine.'

'I must say,' remarked my wife, 'you seem to be very well read.'

'Don't patronize me,' retorted the councillor. 'I've probably read more books than you have, love. I tell you what, the Miners' Welfare has had a much bigger library than the council one, and a better selection of books too. It's a pity that it's getting run down these days, but there you are, the miners today aren't the men they used to be. They are more concerned with the amount of beer they pour down their bellies at the club than what could go into their minds at the Miners' Welfare.'

'Excuse me,' Eleanor replied, 'my father was a miner and I know what the Miners' Welfare did for him. But he didn't want to waste the rest of his life underground and like you he read a great deal. In the end he qualified as a doctor and is still using his knowledge and experience to help others. I can only hope that you are using your knowledge for the benefit of the community as much as he has done.'

The councillor looked at her and then at me. 'I suppose this is your missus. I tell you what, boyo, you've got a good one here. I'm sorry to have been so rude, madam, but from your remark I thought you were one of those who came from a different background, of privilege and of holier and better than thou. I can see that it isn't the case and all I can say is that the vicar here is lucky to have you as his wife.'

I thought the time had come for me to intervene. 'Believe me, Councillor Owen, I know how lucky I am to have Eleanor as my wife. Perhaps I should explain that like her father she is a doctor and is using her knowledge to benefit the community.'

By now the room was empty. 'See what I mean,' said the councillor. 'They have evacuated this place quicker than if there had been an air-raid warning. Well, Doctor, I am sure that you will be a great benefit to the community. I'm not so sure about your husband who is paid to sell the idea that there's pie in the sky when you die. Anyway, I tell you one thing, it's good for Abergwynlais that they've got you two for the next twelve months.'

The Banqueting Hall was a pretentious name for an unadorned large room not much bigger than the church hall in Pontywen. At the far end was the top table and at either end of it two long tables were placed where most of the guests were already seated. A solitary waitress stood by the side of the board and easel which contained the table plan. On her tray there were a few glasses of British sweet sherry. 'All the other's gone,' she said, when we asked for the dry variety.

We made our way down to the top table where we found our places at one end. The mayor's secretary appeared behind me when we sat down. 'The mayor would like you to say grace,' she said.

'With pleasure,' I replied. 'By the way, I wish he had

told me that I was to say a few prayers in the Council Chamber. I would have brought my prayer-book with me in that case.'

'Don't worry, Vicar. You did very well as it was. Perhaps he thought you would know you had to do it, but there you are. I'm afraid he's like that, I should always keep a prayer-book handy if I were you. He's very unpredictable.'

'How exciting,' said my wife when he had gone. 'I would have thought that Dai Spout was extremely predictable, hardly the sort of person of whom you would say, "You never know what he's going to do next."'

'Well, at least next Sunday at the civic service that won't apply,' I remarked. 'The service is printed and I shall be in charge.'

'Wait and see,' replied my wife.

When we arrived back at the vicarage after the reception we found a car parked in the drive and a well-dressed, middle-aged man inspecting the flower border around the lawn.

'Good afternoon, Vicar,' he said. 'I have been trying to get into the church but I found all the doors locked. My name is Powell and I am the parks superintendent for the borough. I must say you have your lawns and borders in good shape. It is a tribute to you.'

'That's due to our excellent gardener, not to me,' I replied. 'What can I do for you?'

'The mayor has asked me to bring some flowers and plants to decorate the church for the civic service on Sunday. This is the first time I have had to do this. So obviously I shall have to look at the interior to work out a colour scheme and where the plants can be seen to best advantage.'

Eleanor looked at me, scarcely able to control her mirth.

'This is news to me, Mr Powell. The mayor has not mentioned it to me, and the lady on the flower rota has probably ordered her flowers for the Sunday.'

'All I can say, Vicar, is that it was news to me this morning when he asked me to make these arrangements. Apparently they used to do it before the war. I think the mayoress is very keen on the idea.'

'I'll go and get the keys for you, dear,' said my wife. She ran around to the back door before she could disgrace herself with unseemly laughter.

'How did the mayor-making go?' inquired Mr Powell. 'I understand there was a sit-down reception this year.'

'There was indeed,' I replied, 'and wine with the dinner, to paraphrase the Duke of Plaza Toro.'

The parks superintendent stared at me. 'Excuse me, Vicar, but who was the Duke of Plaza Toro?'

'A character in *The Gondoliers*, Mr Powell. I am afraid I am a Gilbert and Sullivan addict and I find myself quoting lines from their operas from time to time. We have a church Gilbert and Sullivan Society here in Pontywen, and they are going to perform *The Gondoliers* next year.'

'My wife likes Gilbert and Sullivan, Vicar. She's a bit of a singer, contralto. Mind, she has never done one of their operas, but she has taken part in the musicals in Abergwynlais before the war.'

'That's very interesting,' I replied, 'because Myfanwy Howells, one of our cast, has to back out of our next production because of various other commitments. She is our leading contralto and she would have been playing the Duchess of Plaza Toro – I wonder if your wife would be interested.'

'I am sure she would. She is doing nothing at the moment. I think she would jump at the chance.'

At this stage Eleanor arrived with the keys, smiling broadly.

'Mr Powell has just been telling me that his wife is a contralto who likes Gilbert and Sullivan but never had a chance of performing in one of their operas since her society did other musicals. He thinks she might be interested in doing the Duchess of Plaza Toro, now that Myfanwy Howells has had to withdraw from our show.'

'Marvellous,' said my wife. 'I'll have a word with Aneurin Williams on the phone while you and Mr Powell look round the church. By the time you come back I should be able to give you a message to pass on to your wife, Mr Powell. We rehearse on Thursdays, by the way. Isn't life so unpredictable? You come here at the mayor's request to survey the church and end up by getting your wife a part in *The Gondoliers*.'

As we went up the path to the church, a human scarecrow emerged from behind the gravestones, wearing a battered old trilby, filthy raincoat and even filthier wellington boots. It was 'Full Back' Jones, the gravedigger, whose cadaverous face, unshaven and toothless, could not have been more appropriate for his trade. He coughed loudly to draw attention to himself. The parks superintendent turned around to be confronted with this gruesome sight.

'Sorry to interrupt you, boss,' it lisped, 'but Matthews the Undertaker 'ave been looking for you. It's a re-opening and they wants the funeral as soon as possible. He'll be down to see you tonight but I've got to 'ave a look at the grave plan in the vestry so that I can get on with the job. Walters, the name is, Balaclava Street, 'e says you know the person. You used to bring 'er communion when you was in St Padarn's.'

'Poor old Granny Walters,' I said. 'Of course I knew her. Mr Wentworth-Baxter has been taking her communion since I moved to St Mary's. All right, Full Back, if you go around to the vestry door, I'll open it for you from the inside.'

As he disappeared up the side path, a bewildered Mr Powell inquired, 'Why is he called Full Back?'

'He used to play at full back for Pontywen rugby team many years ago. Apparently he wasn't much good and only played a few games for them but he has never stopped boasting about his brief career. So everybody in Pontywen knows him as Full Back Jones. I am afraid his grave-digging is about as effective as his rugby was.'

Once inside the church, the parks superintendent began to make notes. 'I must say the church is in very good condition, recently redecorated, by the look of it.'

'Yes, we had our centenary last year and the men of the church sacrificed their spare time to celebrate the occasion by giving it a face lift.'

'And a good job they have made of it, Vicar, quite professional. I hope we can do just as good a job with our floral decortications. The mayoress suggested a colour scheme of red and yellow, the Labour Party colours. They should stand out beautifully against the white walls.'

As we moved up into the chancel the vestry door opened and a trilby-hatted gargoyle of a face peered around the door post. 'Boss, I've put the book back.' With that announcement the door was closed.

'I have never seen him without his trilby hat,' I said. 'It is rumoured that he wears it to bed. In that case when he dies it will have to be prised from his head.'

'He is what you would call a character. Life would be all the poorer without them. Well, Vicar, I think I have seen all I want to see. If you don't mind, we shall come here on Saturday afternoon about three o'clock to do our work. I hope you will be happy with it.'

'I am sure I shall be, Mr Powell. I'll have a word with the lady on the flower rota. Don't forget to ask your wife about the part of the Duchess of Plaza Toro. If she is interested we shall be pleased to see her next Thursday evening.'

After I had seen him off, I went into the vicarage to be met by my wife in the hallway. 'You have two visitors in the study. By the expressions on their faces I think it spells trouble. They are large gentlemen. If you need any help, just call for me. I shall be practising my jujitsu in the kitchen. What an exciting day we are having.'

I took a deep breath and opened the study door. Seated in the two armchairs facing my desk were Albert and Arthur Walters, already wearing black armbands to match their black looks.

'I am very sorry to hear about your mother's death,' I said. 'Was it sudden?'

'Sudden,' growled Albert, 'I should think not. She's been on her death-bed for the last three months and nobody has bothered to visit her.'

'Hasn't Mr Wentworth-Baxter been bringing her communion?'

'The last one who brought her communion was you and that was when you were at St Padarn's. Since then nobody has bothered to visit her.'

'I am very sorry about this, Mr Walters. As far as I knew, she was being cared for by the church.'

'The funeral is two o'clock next Friday, if that's suitable for you, Vicar. We don't want nobody else. I'm sure our mother wouldn't either. Mr Matthews said he'll be seeing you later tonight. We'd like to have a service here in St Mary's, if you don't mind. I know she used to go to St Padarn's years ago but since nobody from there has come to see her, we'd rather she was brought into St Mary's.'

'By all means. I shall be able to take the service and perhaps later on you will let me know what hymns you want.'

'I can tell you that now,' intervened Arthur. '"The Lord's my Shepherd" and "Abide with Me". They were her favourites. Whenever they came on the wireless she would be singing them. She knew all the words too.'

They stood up to leave. As I shook hands with Arthur I apologized once again for the church's neglect of their mother. 'Don't worry, Vicar. It's not your fault, we all know that.'

When they had gone, I went into the scullery where Eleanor was doing some ironing. 'You didn't need me then?' she asked.

'Not at all, love. It is Charles's blood they are after. He was supposed to be taking her monthly communion after I moved here and he has not been near her for the whole of that time. Wait till I see him tomorrow.'

'Be careful not to spill blood on our newly cleaned carpet, Frederick. What did Mr Powell have to say?'

'He thinks he will be able to make a fine display of floral decoration in the colours the mayoress has asked for – red and yellow.'

'I see,' said my wife. 'Scarlet to match her hair and yellow to match her teeth.'

'How these women love each other,' I replied.

'You've got it wrong, dear. It's how these Christians love each other.' She giggled and then attacked my pyjama trousers with the iron.

7

'Honestly, Charles, you are incredible. Your sins of omission would fill enough books to stock a library. Ever since you have been in Pontywen you have been more of a liability to the church than an asset. I thought when you married Bronwen that you had changed your ways. This poor old lady was on her death-bed for weeks, completely neglected by the priest who had been given the responsibility to care for her. She died without the last rites of the Church, to which she was entitled. It was fortunate for you that the family has insisted that I take the funeral. Had it been you who had to officiate you would have felt the lash of their tongues.'

He sat with his head bowed, a familiar sight which had been repeated in the vicarage study several times over the past three years – that and the usual wounded spaniel expression on his face when he did raise his head.

'Sorry, Fred. What happened was this: I had forgotten all about Mrs Walters for some reason or another and then when I did remember a few weeks ago, I felt too embarrassed to call there after such a gap.'

'That makes matters even worse. It was not just amnesia but a bout of cowardice as well. As an act of penance you will have to play the organ at the service in St Mary's. Eric Greenfield can't get away from work to play at the funeral. I should keep a low profile if I were you, otherwise there might be a gap in your teeth. Those big men in the Walters family are very handy with their fists, so I hear.' The colour drained from his face.

The old lady's husband had died in an accident at the Pontywen Colliery in 1919, leaving her with a family of five boys and three girls to bring up on the pitifully small compensation she was given, plus her widow's pension. In the small terraced house in Balaclava Street she reared her children to adulthood in a way which earned her the respect of her neighbours as well as that of her family. She was a supreme example of the Welsh matriarch. She made sure that none of her sons would have to work underground. Four of them were employed in the steel-works and the youngest joined the army when he was seventeen. The eight children worshipped their mother who was nursed through her illness by her eldest daughter, the only one of the family who still lived in the house where they had all been born.

Friday turned out to be a hot summer's day. 'Gentlemen only at the church and graveside' read the announcements in the evening paper. When I arrived at 11 Balaclava Street for the service in the house, I was ushered into the middle room by Albert Walters. 'Have a drop of something before you start, Vicar.' He handed me a tumbler which was half-filled with whisky.

Already the house was crammed with mourners. The smell of mothballs and cheap perfume mingled with the body odour of sweating humanity, whilst from the open door of the front room which had sheltered the death-bed of the old lady emanated distinct evidence of disinfectant. It was a powerful concoction which combined with the whisky to make my head spin by the time I was ready to take the service in the front room. Everybody had to stand. There was no room for chairs.

'Anybody want to see Mrs Walters before we screw the coffin down?' bellowed the undertaker, Mr Matthews, from upstairs. For someone in his profession he was singularly devoid of any sensitivity. He was at his best as a carpenter. No one wished to take advantage of his offer. In any case it would have been extremely difficult for anyone to squeeze through the scrum of humanity to make the journey upstairs to view the mortal remains.

'We shall begin our service with a reading from the seventh chapter of the Book of Revelation. "After this I beheld and lo, a great multitude which no man could number."' The first vocal signs of grief were heard. By the time I came to the last verse of the lesson: 'And God shall wipe away tears from their eyes', there was a torrent of tears from all the daughters and the daughters-in-law which continued throughout Psalm 23. I was seized in the grip of a violent attack of claustrophobia. 'Shall we say together the Lord's Prayer?' I found myself saying. Breathing was becoming difficult for me. I felt as if I was about to faint.

'Two quick prayers,' I said to myself while everybody else was saying the Lord's Prayer. 'O Lord, we pray for those whom we love but see no longer.' A loud wail arose from Meg, the eldest daughter. I competed with her for audibility throughout the prayer, a competition which she won with ease as I found myself gasping for breath. 'I've got to finish now,' I ordered myself. 'The blessing of God Almighty be with us all, now and always,' I para-phrased. I closed my eyes for a few seconds. When I opened them the room appeared to be going around in circles. 'Would you excuse me,' I said to Meg, 'but I have to get back to the church to see that everything is ready for the service. I'll see you next week.'

A path was made for me among the mourners. As I emerged from the throng in the doorway I had never known the polluted air of Pontywen to be as welcome. I stood and took gulps of air as if I were drinking the best champagne. One of the drivers opened the front door of an ancient limousine for me. 'No, thank you.' I said. 'I shall walk on. By the time you leave here, I shall be in the church.'

When I arrived at St Mary's, I was met by the strains of 'Crimond' being played by Charles at the organ. As an organist he was a splendid pianist. He had no idea of how to use the foot pedals but he made up for that deficiency by playing the keyboard accurately and using the organ stops judiciously.

'You can stop that, Charles,' I said, tapping him on the shoulder and causing him to crash into a discord from fright. 'I didn't hear you come in,' he gasped.

'You could have put hymn-books and prayer-books out in the pews before you started on the organ. And before you say "Sorry" for the thousandth time you had better get cracking now before the mourners arrive. I don't think the Walters crowd want to see you.'

He was off the organ seat and down the aisle as if his life depended on it. Then, gathering up armfuls of books, he was running towards the front pews and dropping several as he went. By the time he had finished, he was sweating profusely and panting like an overweight prop forward after a run across the field.

'Just in time,' I said, as I walked down towards the door at the west end. 'I can hear the hearse drawing up.'

A few minutes later the cortege, led by myself reciting the burial verses in the Book of Common Prayer, made its way down the aisle to the foot of the chancel where I had placed the trestles to await the arrival of the coffin. Charles was featuring the vox angelica organ stop in a quiet, tremulous rendering of Mendelssohn's 'O Rest in the Lord' while the undertaker's sergeant-major tones barked out instructions to the four Walters brothers who were acting as bearers. 'Careful now. Mind what you're doing. Thank you, gentlemen.' At the back of the church friends and neighbours of the male gender filed into the pews while Mr Matthews loudly directed the family into the front pews.

I waited for the master of ceremonies to retire to the west end of the church before announcing the first hymn, 'The Lord's my Shepherd', played somewhat tentatively by the nervous curate but sung with fervour by the scratch male voice choir. When that ended I announced that we would say Psalm 90 in alternate verses. It turned out to be a solo recitation by the vicar because Charles was too frightened to make his voice heard at the organ and the congregation were reluctant to join in. However, they were prepared to co-operate in the saying of the Lord's Prayer and in a rousing rendition of 'Guide Me, O Thou Great Redeemer' to the tune of 'Cwm Rhondda', something they had often sung in pubs, bus outings and twice a year at Cardiff Arms Park.

At the end of the service we had to wait for some more military manoeuvres with the coffin supervised by RSM Matthews before we emerged from the church into the afternoon sunlight. My head had cleared and I felt at peace with the world. I was leading the coffin containing the body of a servant of God to its last resting-place. In the distance I could see the familiar sight of Full Back Jones standing by the newly dug grave, ready to sprinkle the earth over the coffin when it was laid in the ground.

The only sound to be heard was the crunch of gravel made by the feet of the bearers and the mourners. We came to a halt opposite the waiting grave-digger.

Suddenly the silence was shattered by a shout – 'This is the wrong grave.' It was Albert Walters, one of the two leading bearers who were standing with their mother's coffin weighing heavily on their shoulders. 'Put the coffin down,' ordered the undertaker. By now the air was filled with a hubbub of voices as loud as any when last orders were called at the Workingmen's Club.

'Where is the right one, then?' demanded Mr Matthews.

'Over by there, next to that headstone,' replied Albert. 'I used to come here with my mother when I was a kid. It had a wooden cross on it then but that's gone ages ago. We were going to 'ave it replaced but never got round to it.'

'The first thing to do is to go to the vestry to check the grave number,' I said. 'It's not like Full Back to make a mistake like this.'

'Well, according to the register, boss, the grave is F8,' interjected the grave-digger, 'double depth.'

'There's only one way to find out. Mr Matthews and Mr Walters, will you come with me to the vestry, please?' I asked, 'And will everyone else please stay where you are for the time being?' When we arrived at the vestry I opened the register with trembling fingers to find the page with the all-important number. Eventually I turned the entry for 17 January 1918, 'Albert Joseph Walters, age 37', and along-side in the margin 'F6'. It could have been mistaken for F8 because the curl at the end of the six at the top almost reached the bottom half of the figure, but there was no doubt that Full Back Jones had dug the wrong grave.

'What did I tell you?' said Albert. 'Now what do we do? We've got all the refreshments and that in the house. We can't ask everybody to come back tomorrow.'

'I'm afraid that is exactly what you will have to do. In no way will the grave-digger be able to open up the grave ready for burial today. I'm terribly sorry that this has happened. As you can see, it was a mistake which anybody could have made. If there had been a headstone or wooden cross on the grave this would never happened.'

'I tell you what, Vicar. After the way my mother was treated when she was alive and now when she's dead, the church 'as 'ad it, as far as I'm concerned, and I'm sure that will go for the rest of the family, I can tell you.'

Since none of the Walters family ever came to church it would have made no difference to the attendance figures whatsoever.

'It will have to be at three-thirty, Vicar,' said the undertaker. 'We've got a two o'clock at Moriah churchyard and you know how long they go on. So we'll meet you at the church then. What about the coffin? Do you want us to take it back to the house?'

'Not at all,' I replied, 'let the body rest in peace in the church. That will compensate for all the mayhem this afternoon. I suppose that's all right with you, Mr Walters. I'm sure it would upset your sisters and your wives if your mother's body came back to the house.'

'You're telling me, Vicar. It will be bad enough as it is without having my mother going back and fore like a yo-yo. I think it's disgraceful in any case. I tell you what, you haven't heard the last of this. I'll be writing to the paper for a start.'

'You do what you like, Mr Walters, but I'm sure your mother would not want a big fuss made about what has happened. She was a very dear lady who never said an unkind word about anybody. In the meanwhile I suggest that we go back and inform everybody about the new arrangement. The sooner your mother's mortal remains are taken back into the peace of the church the better.'

I closed the register and ushered the two men out of the vestry, apprehensive about the reaction of the waiting mourners. Albert raced back with the news that he was right about the grave. By the time I arrived at the wrongly dug grave, I was faced with an angry mob who minutes ago were the silent mourners. For the first time in my life I appreciated what Daniel must have felt in his predicament in the lions' den. In the meanwhile Full Back Jones had retreated behind a large gravestone, prepared to stay out of sight until the coast was clear.

'Gentlemen!' I shouted. 'I must apologize for this unfortunate happening. Since the grave was unmarked, the Sexton had to consult the register in the vestry. The grave number at first sight looked like F8 and that is the grave which he opened. However, when we examined the number a few minutes ago, it transpired that the number was F6.'

'Why couldn't it have transpired to Full Back that it was F6?' demanded Arthur Walters.

'Your brother will tell you, Mr Walters, that it was very difficult to tell the difference. Anyway, under the circumstances, I have to inform you that we shall meet at the church tomorrow at three-thirty when the burial will take place in the correct grave. In the meanwhile the body of the late Mrs Walters will lie at rest in the church until then. Once again I apologize for all the inconvenience involved and I hope that you all will be able to meet here tomorrow afternoon to pay your last respects to someone who was a true Christian in every meaning of that word. We shall say a few prayers in the church and then go to the graveside.'

My words seemed to have stilled the storm of protest. The Walters brothers once again carried the coffin on their shoulders into the church, only to find that my curate, in an unusual display of zeal, had taken the trestles back into the vestry. By now the bearers were showing signs of exhaustion. It had been a long walk from the grave. The undertaker had offered the services of his trolley for the funeral, but the men had insisted they wanted to carry their mother's body.

As Mr Matthews and I made our way to retrieve the missing support for the coffin, he said to me, 'I'll bring my trolley tomorrow. I bet they'll be glad of it. They'll have sore shoulders for a week after this.' When we entered the vestry there was no sign of the trestles in the alcove where they were kept. I opened the curtains which covered the cassocks and surplices but the stands were not there. Charles had struck again.

'Perhaps you had better go back into the church and suggest that they rest the coffin on top of the front pews, Mr Matthews, otherwise they will be in no fit state to attend the burial tomorrow.' The undertaker disappeared immediately. As I surveyed the vestry, I racked my brains for a solution to the mystery of the missing trestles. Then the vestry door opened. It was Full Back Jones.

'I thought you wanted them trestles in the church again. So what are they doing outside the door? I was coming back for my wheelbarrow from the boiler-'ouse when I saw them. I'm sorry for the mess-up about the graves, boss, but I could 'ave swore that was number eight. I'll 'ave to work like the clappers now to get that grave done for tomorrow.'

'That's all right, Full Back. You get back to that new grave and I'll get these trestles back where they are needed.' The thought of Full Back Jones working 'like the clappers' was as unlikely as Charles Wentworth-Baxter doing the same in his parochial duties. They were like 'two lovely berries moulded on one stem' in that respect, but certainly in no other.

Carrying the trestles on either arm, I staggered into the chancel to be met with glares from the Walters contingent. The undertaker managed to meet me and to take one of the trestles. 'You should have called me, Vicar,' he said.

When the trestles were in place, the brothers lowered the coffin to its resting place and then departed quickly from the scene, relieved from their burden and anxious to return to the house and the refreshments. In the meanwhile, the driver of the hearse began to bring the wreaths and cut flowers into the chancel. It was then that I remembered the church was to be invaded by the Parks Department at about the same time that the mourners would be entering the church for the few prayers. A dozen dire scenarios flooded into my mind. The mayoress, who was coming to inspect the decorations, would take it that the coffin in the midst of her red and yellow flowers was a bad omen for her year of office. The Walters family would resent the intrusion of the council workmen into the solemnity of their mother's funeral, and make another protest. Mourners would be colliding with the decorators who would be rushing to get the Saturday chore over as soon as possible.

I went back to the vicarage and sat in the armchair in my study, hunched up in despair. At this late stage I could hardly expect the parks superintendent to change his arrangements. On the other hand, to change the time of the funeral would be to invite a shower of coals of fire on my head from the Walters family. I realized the agony that Mr Hobson felt when he had to make his choice. The sound of Eleanor's car coming down the drive roused me from my melancholy. Thank God for Henry the Eighth and the marriage of the clergy he brought about, I said to myself, even if he had more than his fair share of wives. I arose from the armchair and went to meet her at the door, greeting her with a kiss.

'What's that all about?' she inquired. 'If it's cupboard love, I am afraid you will have to wait quite a while. I am expecting a full surgery at five o'clock. If it is not cupboard love, then by the look on your face it is a tale of woe and you have just a quarter of an hour to tell Eleanor.'

We moved into the sitting-room where she sat down on the settee and patted the cushion beside her. 'I am sitting comfortably,' she said, quoting the presenters' words on the new children's programme on the wireless. 'So you can begin, but cut it short, there's a dear.'

By the time I had finished my account of the afternoon's events she was convulsed with laughter. 'It's no laughing matter, love. It's a whole series of catastrophes. There's poor old Granny Walters who should be resting in her grave in peace, hanging about in the chancel and holding up the preparations for the civic service, not to mention her family who are in militant mood, to say the least.'

'Fred, my love,' replied my wife, 'poor old Granny Walters is looking down from above and feeling very important at being able to feature in the Dai Spout saga just before his moment of glory. She could never have had such prominence if she were still confined to her bed in Balaclava Street. I don't see why you can't ring up the parks superintendent and ask him if he could either come earlier with his workmen or later, as the case may be. It is just one of those things that happen. Go and ring him now. He should still be in his office. If he is not, then you can get someone there to ask him to ring you as soon as possible.'

I went into my study, found the Parks Department number and dialled it nervously. There was an instant reply. 'Can I speak to the superintendent, please?' I asked. 'Speaking,' said the voice.

'This is Fred Secombe. I am afraid that there has been an unexpected hitch in the arrangements for the decoration of the church tomorrow afternoon. You see, at the time when you are due to start your activities, there is a body in the church and there will be mourners there for a short service a little later.'

'I see,' said the voice, 'but why didn't you tell me this when we arranged the time?'

'Well, the funeral should have taken place this afternoon, but unfortunately it has had to be postponed until tomorrow and the undertaker cannot come earlier because he has already arranged a funeral at Moriah Chapel earlier in the afternoon. The – er – truth is that the gravedigger dug the wrong grave.'

There was a long pause and a bout of coughing at the other end of the phone.

'I am sorry about that, Vicar. I shall contact my men immediately and arrange for them to begin earlier tomorrow morning. We shall be in the church at 11 a.m, if that suits you.'

'That is fine by me. I hope the coffin on its stand and the flowers placed around it will not interfere with your preparations.'

'Not at all, Vicar. Its presence will help to keep the noise down while they work. There won't be much shouting tomorrow, I can tell you. I shall let the mayoress know of the change in time. If she can't make it, I'm afraid that's just too bad. By the way, how did the grave-digger come to dig the wrong grave?'

'It's a long story, I'm afraid, and is best summed up by saying he didn't know a six from an eight.'

'Well, having had a glimpse of him I am not at all surprised. He looks as if he doesn't know what soap and water is, either.'

When I went into the sitting-room, my beloved said, 'By the look on your face, it would seem that all is well. What would you do without me, your acting unpaid assistant? Talking of which, isn't it great that I shall be having my acting paid assistant with me on Monday? No more unreliable locums and more time to spend with you, love.' She jumped up, kissed me lightly on the lips and waltzed out of the room. In no time at all, her car was on its way up the drive.

Next morning Charles and I were joined by Granny Walters for our service. 'It's a bit eerie having the coffin up here in the chancel with us,' said my curate.

'The only reply to that is that at least she is having your company in death, if she didn't have it in life, and don't forget to remember her in the prayers after the third collect.'

Before we could reach that point, there was a loud banging on the vestry door. 'Hold on, Charles,' I said. 'I expect that is Full Back. Only he could be making enough noise to wake the dead.' I went into the vestry and opened the door.

'Boss, I've put the blessed pick through my foot.' He

pointed down to the instep of his filthy wellington boot. Blood was oozing through a hole.

'Stay there,' I said. 'I'll bring my wife along straight-away. Charles, get a chair for him.'

I ran back to the vicarage. Eleanor was in her dressing-gown in the kitchen, making a cup of tea.

'What on earth is the matter?' she said.

'Full Back has put a pick through his foot,' I gasped.

'Get the car out of the garage while I do a quick change,' she ordered. By the time I had manoeuvred the car to the front of the house, she was dressed and was carrying her medical bag with her.

'Heaven knows what infection has got into that foot, knowing his unwashed state,' she said. 'Obviously he will have to be taken to the hospital and given penicillin as soon as possible.'

When we arrived outside the vestry, Charles was look-ing paler than the patient whose face was so dirty that it was difficult to tell the state of his complexion. 'Sorry about this, boss,' said Full Back. 'What's going to 'appen with the grave?'

'Never mind about the grave, let's get that wellington off so that the doctor can have a look at your foot.'

'I'll get the boot off,' said my wife. When she removed it, the sight of the blood streaming from the wound combined with the smell of his unwashed foot turned my stomach. Charles had disappeared into the vestry, unable to cope with the unveiling of Full Back's injury.

In no time at all Eleanor had placed a piece of lint and a piece of cotton-wool on the foot and bound them tightly with a roll of bandage. She took me aside into the vestry where my curate was sitting at my desk with a vacant expression on his face, obviously overwhelmed by

the occasion. 'Stage one,' she said. 'The next thing is to get him to the vicarage and bathe the wound. Fred, you had better phone the hospital casualty ward and prepare them for the emergency treatment. I think he has broken the bone but the most important thing at the moment is to kill the infection. Otherwise it will not be a broken bone to worry about but septicaemia and the prospect of him losing his leg. Charles, you and Fred get on either side of him. Then, when I have turned the car around, get him into the back with his leg on the seat.'

I had never been in such close proximity to the grave-digger, whose lack of personal hygiene generated enough aroma to rival anything the local pig farm could supply. Charles's complexion had now progressed from white to green. In the meanwhile Full Back Jones was suffering so much pain that his language in my presence knew no restraint. 'Blessed' had become 'bloody', and his foot was hurting like 'buggery' instead of like 'blazes'.

When Eleanor had ministered to his immediate needs in the vicarage she drove off in her car with him to the hospital, leaving me to find someone to dig the grave for the afternoon's burial. As far as I could see, the only hope I had was to contact Tom Cadwallader, the sexton at Llanhyfryd Church. Tom was a giant of a man and would be able to do the job in the short time available. However, his humble cottage was devoid of a telephone, as it was of electricity and other modern conveniences.

My ancient Morris Minor made the journey to Llanhyfryd at a speed which cut at least ten minutes off my average for the three-mile run. When I arrived at the cottage, his wife was on the gate in earnest conversation with Miss Owen who presided at the harmonium in the parish church. 'You're in a hurry, Vicar,' said Mrs Cadwallader, startled by the screech of brakes and my rapid emergence from the vehicle.

'Where's Tom?' I asked.

'He's down in the bottom of the garden getting some of his compost heap for his kidney beans,' she replied.

'I've got to see him at once,' I said. She took a few steps down the path and shouted, 'Tom!' It was loud enough to be heard back in Pontywen. To my intense relief the burly figure of her husband ambled up the path.

'You're up here early, Vicar.' The very slowness of his speech had a calming influence on the turbulence in my head.

'Can you do a job for me urgently? In fact, straight-away.'

He looked at one quizzically.

'What job is that, Vicar?'

'Digging a grave in Pontywen Churchyard ready for a burial this afternoon.' There was a long pause while his brain came to terms with my request.

'Where's Full Back Jones, then?'

'He's been taken to hospital. He put a pick through his foot.'

'Nasty,' he said. Tom was a man of few words. 'You want me to come now, then?'

'Yes, please.'

'What about his dinner?' asked Mrs Cadwallader.

'I'll see he gets something to eat at the vicarage. I'll bring him back as soon as he has filled the grave in. I'm afraid it won't be until about five o'clock.'

'Well, that's his Saturday gone,' she said crossly.

'I was only going to be in the garden, woman,' said her husband. That was the longest sentence he spoke for the rest of the time he was in my presence that day.

8

'He's a lucky man,' said Eleanor. 'The X-ray shows no break in the bone but there is severe bruising. The doctor thinks his wellingtons were thick enough to prevent any further injury.'

I met her as she was on her way out to take her surgery. Tom Cadwallader was now busily engaged opening up the grave, only too happy that Pontywen Churchyard was free of the rock which was to be found in parts of Llanhyfryd Churchyard. There had been one famous occasion not long after my arrival in the parish when he used dynamite as a last resort to open up a grave. Unfortunately it had been when the mourners were already in church for the service. The loud blast which ensued was like the Last Trump and coincided with my reading of the burial lesson. 'The trumpet shall sound and the dead shall arise.' There has never been a more startled congregation than that one, not to mention the clergyman. I was unable to continue the lesson for quite a while.

'Mrs Cadwallader is worried that her husband will be without food. So I have told her that we shall give him something to eat, forgetting that Mrs Watkins will not be here today because it's Saturday, I hope you don't mind.'

'Fear not, Frederick, and all will be well. I shall pick up some fish and chips on my way back from my visits. All you have to do is to put the oven on at about a quarter to one. I would suggest that you get a bottle of beer for Tom. He is bound to be very thirsty, excavating in this warm weather. Perhaps a barrel would be more appropriate by the look of his girth. By the way, there's one good thing about Full Back's stay in hospital. He will come out so clean that people in Pontywen won't know him.'

'Give him a month back home and he will soon be recognizable. Anyway, he will be anxious to be up and about as soon as possible. He will not want Tom Cadwallader to be invading his patch if he can help it.'

'I must be off, love. I'm late for my surgery as it is. You can get on with your epic for tomorrow. Don't forget you have the whole of the council at your mercy. So sock it to 'em, kid.'

'Very elegant encouragement, I must say, from a vicar's wife.'

'Oh, shut up! Give us a kiss and let me go to my duties.'

I granted her request and watched her shoot up the drive like a latter-day Malcolm Campbell.

As I went back into the house, I thought over what she had said. I had intended to preach an innocuous sermon based on the parable of the Good Samaritan, stressing that councillors had to be good neighbours to all the citizens whom they represented. However, since the little conversation with Bill Moscow and his hint of corruption in the town hall I had felt more than a little disturbed. Occasionally I had heard tales of school-teachers bribing councillors to secure a headmaster's job for them but I had regarded such rumours as tittle-tattle. The Communist's words indicated that bribes were not confined to the sphere of education but extended to building contracts as well.

In the study, I began to thumb through the Epistles to find a suitable text and in no time at all I found what I wanted. It was as if I had been led by the Spirit to find it, St Paul's Epistle to the Romans, the thirteenth verse of the thirteenth chapter: 'Let us walk honestly as in the day.' Although I was unaccustomed to praying in public without the use of a prayer-book, my sermons were always preached without notes. I had thought of writing out my civic service sermon, but now I felt that I could best achieve my objective by my usual method of looking at the congregation and addressing them face to face, without the impediment of being tied to 'a piece of paper', as Dai Spout had put it.

After an hour of reading through commentaries on the Epistle and some essays on Church and State, I subsided into an armchair to sort out my thoughts. My musings were interrupted by a ring on the doorbell. It was the parks superintendent.

'Excuse me, Vicar. I should like your advice on the decoration of the end of the church where you have the altar. I know you won't like it too cluttered up because of your communion service in the morning. I hope I have not interrupted you in your work, but we have finished in the body of the church and I would like to let the men get away for what's left of their Saturday. They weren't overjoyed when they knew they had to work today, I can tell you.'

'I'm sure they weren't. I'm in the middle of preparing my sermon for tomorrow. Still, a break will do me a power of good. Has the mayoress been to see the decorations?'

'She was going to come for a few minutes to inspect the work when it was done. Then when she heard that there was a coffin in the church, she changed her mind. She said it would be a bad omen for her to see it.'

'I thought it might have that effect on her. Well, the old lady inside it would be the last to put a curse on anyone. To talk of much lighter things, Mr Powell, is your good lady looking forward to joining us for *The Gondoliers*?'

'By the way, Vicar, my name is Hugh. Yes, Rhoda is quite excited about it. She says it's the only chance she will ever have of becoming a Duchess. So she may as well make the most of it.'

When we entered the church, it was like a visit to the Chelsea Flower Show. The window-sills, the ends of the pews and the font were ablaze with red and yellow flowers. At the foot of the lectern were pots of red geraniums. The only clash of colour was in the chancel where Granny Walters' coffin lay surmounted by a massive wreath forming the word 'Mam' in white carnations and surrounded by wreaths in colours of all kinds.

'I thought we had better leave the choir stalls alone because of the coffin and the wreaths. So we ought to have a splash of colour on the altar and on either side of it. I've got some red and yellow roses for the vases on the altar and I wondered whether I might put a few pots of geraniums at the back where they would not be in your way at the communion service tomorrow morning.'

'That will be fine, Hugh. My name is Fred. So please drop the "Vicar" bit from now on. Yes, I think you have done the church proud. I doubt if it will ever look as splendid as it is now. The congregation at tomorrow morning's service are in for a delightful surprise.'

'We'll remove the pots of flowers on Monday morning but the cut flowers are yours until they fade away. It's up to you, Fred, to do what you like with them.'

'There's only one answer to that. On Sunday evening we shall bunch them up and take them to the housebound members of the congregation who will be thrilled to have them.'

I left Hugh Powell in the church supervising the adornment of the sanctuary and went into the churchyard to see how the stand-in grave-digger was progressing with his labours. To my amazement there were now two large mounds of earth on either side of the opening and the only indication of Tom's presence was the loud grunt which accompanied each spadeful of soil. When I reached the grave, he was several feet down.

'Nearly finished, Vicar,' he said.

'Well done!' I replied. 'It takes Full Back half a day just to dig a few feet down. Would you like me to drive you home now, and pick you up later to fill in the grave?'

'No, thanks. Better stay here now. Do a bit of tidying up that long grass.'

'In that case, you can have some fish and chips at one o'clock and a bottle of beer to go with it.' He wiped away the sweat which was streaming down his ruddy countenance and almost smiled. The thought of being apart from Mrs Cadwallader for the next four or five hours and being fed and adequately watered had made his day.

As I was emerging from the jug and bottle department of the Lamb and Fly, with a carrier bag laden with half a dozen small bottles of the local brew, I was confronted by Bertie Owen, a militant shop steward in matters ecclesiastical as well as industrial. 'Why haven't any of the sidesmen from St Padarn's been invited to help at the civic service in St Mary's? After all, it's something that concerns the whole parish, not just the favoured few up there. I tell you what, if I had still been churchwarden you would have known about it by now.'

'I'm sure I would have, Bertie, but as you are not churchwarden I don't see that it's any business of yours. Obviously you don't know it, but I have asked both the wardens from St Padarn's to come and help at the service. Since we only need six sidesmen at most to hand out the service forms, it is pointless having any more present. They would be falling over each other. You will be very welcome to attend the service even if your help isn't needed.'

'Then, what about this business of Mrs Walters going to be buried in the wrong grave and the curate not coming to see her?'

'Bertie, you really are an old applewoman. If you think anything of your church, you had better stop going around and stirring up trouble. It's small wonder that the congregation replaced you at the last Easter Vestry.'

'That's all you can say after everything I've done for St Padarn's. Well!' He turned on his heels and strode off.

When Eleanor came in with the fish and chips from Cascarni's, I told her about the encounter with Bertie. 'What did you expect, love?' she said. 'Obviously the Walters family are going to broadcast their grievances as much as possible, and who better to do their broadcasting for them than Bertie Owen? As for the sidesmen required for the service tomorrow, only he could make a fuss about that. He's just frustrated that he can't be there bossing everybody about. You had better go across and get Tom to come for his victuals. Far better to have his silent fellowship than Bertie's backchat.'

I found him in a corner of the churchyard, wielding a scythe in the heat of the day. 'This could do with sharpening, Vicar,' he commented.

'I don't doubt that, Tom. Full Back very rarely used it. He is only too pleased to have Jones Blaenycwm's sheep in here to keep the grass down.'

'I'll take it home and sharpen it.'

'Never mind about that for the time being. Come and have some food and drink.'

As Eleanor forecast, we did all the talking while Tom concentrated on eating and drinking. By the time the meal was over he had emptied four bottles of best bitter. It was a happy man who went back to the grass-cutting.

We were in the sitting-room enjoying a gin and tonic when an MG two-seater pre-war model made a noisy entrance down the drive. In it was a young man in a sports jacket and open-necked shirt, plus cravat, and a young lady in a bright summery dress. They were out of the car in a trice as if on urgent business.

I went to the door and opened it just as the young man was about to press the button.

'Don't tell me, Vicar. You saw us come down the drive.'

'To be more exact, I heard you come down the drive and then I saw you.'

'It is rather noisy, I must admit. I am Gareth Andrews and this is my fiancée, Heather Francis. My apologies for intruding upon you but it was such a nice day that I thought it would be a good idea to bring Heather with me to see the place where I shall be working.'

By now, Eleanor had joined me on the doorstep. 'Welcome, partner, or should I say "pard", and welcome, too, to the pardess.'

There was much hand-shaking all round. Gareth Andrews was at least some five inches taller than my five foot seven, whilst Heather was about the same height as

Eleanor in the five foot region. He was dark-haired and sported a luxuriant black moustache whilst his fiancée was a platinum blonde. They made a handsome couple.

'Please come in. We are just enjoying a gin and tonic. I am about to take a funeral in an hour or so's time and the gin is the only strong drink which will not taint my breath. Would you care to join us?'

'By all means,' said Heather. 'It is my one and only drink. That doesn't go for Gareth but he's omnivorous, anyway.'

In no time at all, we were a happy and congenial quartet. I was very glad for my wife who had been coping with a burgeoning practice, completely reliant on a mixed bag of locums for help, some of whom were not as competent as they might have been. I filled their glasses and suggested a toast. 'To the new era in the Pontywen medical history and long may it prosper.'

'Come off it, boss,' said my beloved. 'I should be doing that, not you. You can do that for your next change of curate, whenever that may be. Anyway, I second what he has said.'

We raised our glasses and drank, not as deeply as Tom Cadwallader but just as satisfactorily.

Time went by very quickly. Gareth and Heather talked about their wedding plans and their need to find a home in Pontywen. Eleanor gave Gareth a rough picture of what was involved in the practice with its preponderance of lung complaints. I looked at my watch. The funeral was due in quarter of an hour's time.

'I'm afraid I have to go now,' I said, 'but I should be back in half an hour or so. There are just a few prayers to be said in church and then the committal.'

Gareth stood up. 'Do you mind if I come across to the

123

church with you? My uncle is an incumbent in the Hereford diocese and I have spent many happy hours at his rectory. I'd like to have a look at your church since I shall be worshipping there before long. In any case it will give the two girls an opportunity for a natter.'

As we walked up the church path I suggested to him that he could have a look inside the church while I went to see Tom Cadwallader to check if everything was ready for the burial. There was no sign of his burly figure anywhere. I went up to the far end of the churchyard where he had been wielding the scythe. There was neither sight nor sound of any activity. On the way back to the grave, I heard a sound, a sound of inactivity. It came from behind a large gravestone, a loud snore. The Llanhyfryd sexton was sprawled out in careless abandon, with the blade of the scythe in perilous proximity to his scarlet moon of a face. Like Granny Walters, he was at peace with the world, but unlike her he was soon to awake to the harsh reality of life. Carefully I removed the scythe from its place, then I caught hold of him and shouted, 'Wake up, Tom.' There was not even a flicker of an eyelid. The snores grew louder. It was evident that the four bottles of beer and the heat of the sun had anaesthetized him as effectively as any patient in the operating theatre of Pontywen Hospital.

I ran rather than walked to the church. Gareth was standing in the nave surrounded by the red and yellow flowers, admiring the east window of the church installed in 1925 in memory of Sir David Jones-Williams' father. It depicted the manger scene at Bethlehem, where the three kings with their gifts were supplemented by three miners with helmeted head-lamps, apparently brought there by courtesy of the colliery owner who had exploited them.

'Gareth!' I gasped. 'I'm in trouble. The grave-digger who should be at the interment sprinkling the earth on the coffin and, more importantly, filling in the grave afterwards is lying behind a grave dead drunk.'

'That's terrible,' he said. 'You'll have to sack him. He can't come to do his job in that state, it's unbelievable.'

'It's believable, all right,' I replied, 'because I gave him the four bottles of beer which caused it. My main concern at the moment is the funeral which is due any minute now.'

He looked at me as if I were as drunk as Tom Ca l-wallader.

'I'll explain later,' I went on, 'but how can I get him round?'

'My dear Vicar, you can't get him round immediately to say the least. Why don't I divest myself of this jacket and leave it in the vestry? I'll get the handfuls of earth and do the sprinkling. If we can't bring him round to normality, I'll fill in the grave. I know what to do. I've seen it done often enough during the war. As for the sprinkling that comes with the earth to earth, ashes to ashes, dust to dust bit, leave it to me.'

By the time I had robed, the funeral cortege was arriving at the churchyard gates. I went out to meet them. The undertaker came up to me. 'Straight out into the churchyard, Vicar?'

'A few prayers in church first, Mr Matthews.'

'As you say, Vicar. I just thought that as we've already had the service, there was no need for anything else.'

The drivers opened the car doors for the mourners to alight. There was obvious hostility on the faces of the mourners who felt that they were in some kind of unnecessary replay with no worthwhile jamboree to compensate for it afterwards.

I went on ahead into the church and took my place in my stall ready to read the prayers. Opposite me, out of sight of the mourners, Gareth stood at the side of the organ, now minus his jacket but not his cravat. He gave me the thumbs-up sign, presumably for my encouragement. I felt as if I were in some kind of bizarre pantomime, rather than at Granny Walters' funeral.

One by one the mourners shuffled down the aisle and into the pews where they surveyed the floral decorations with some bewilderment. When they were all seated I stood up to address them. 'I am very sorry that you have had to come back here for the second time. I understand fully the distress you must feel as a result. We shall say a few prayers for the repose of the soul of Elizabeth Walters and then proceed to the graveside for the burial. Let us pray.'

The mourners slumped forward in the pews in what has been described as 'the shampoo position' and mumbled the Lord's Prayer. After the reading of the prayers, I moved down the nave and waited to lead the cortege out into the churchyard. Mr Matthews removed the wreaths from around the coffin and then in his sergeant-major voice gave instructions to the Walters brothers for the carrying of the coffin. After a number of manoeuvres they began to bear their mother's body down the aisle. As we came out of the church and walked down the central path of the churchyard, I could see Gareth in the distance, his shirt-sleeves rolled up, obviously ready for business. When we reached the graveside he was standing behind a neighbouring gravestone, keeping a watch on the proceedings. 'Man that is born of woman has but a short time to live,' I intoned, as we moved from the path to the grave which had been dug deeper and far more neatly than anything Full Back had done since I was in Pontywen. I motioned to Gareth to come forward before I said the words of committal. When his tall figure appeared beside me clad in expensively cut trousers and a silk cravat adorning his open-necked shirt, carrying a handful of earth, the undertaker and the bearers stopped in their tracks, paralysed by astonishment. There could not have been a greater contrast between the filthy appearance of the bearer of the earth yesterday and what they witnessed now.

Mr Matthews recovered his composure: 'Thread the webbing through the 'andles, gentlemen. Right. Now when you stand on the plank, wait for me to say "lower" before you start and don't forget to lower gently. Hang on to the webbing after you've lowered, don't forget. Then leave the ends on the planks.' When the brothers had complied with his instructions and the coffin lay in its place, I began the words of the committal. 'For as much as it hath pleased Almighty God of his great mercy to take unto himself the soul of our dear sister here departed, we therefore commit her body to the ground.' I nodded to Gareth who stepped forward smartly and collided with Albert Walters who would have joined his mother had it not been for the intervention of Arthur, who pulled him back from the brink.

'Sorry, old man,' said the volunteer sexton, as the two brothers glared at him.

'Earth to earth,' I went on, and a shower of small stones and clay thudded on the coffin. 'Ashes to ashes', and another fusillade followed. 'Dust to dust', and by now Gareth had run out of ammunition and an anticlimax of a small plop resulted. 'You can move back now,' I whispered to him. 'Apologies for running out of earth,' he whispered in reply.

'In sure and certain hope of the Resurrection to Eternal Life,' I continued, uninterrupted for the rest of the service. By the time the prayers ended, Gareth had disappeared. I shook hands with mourners who then spent five minutes looking at the wreaths that the two drivers had brought from the church. In the meanwhile I was approached by the undertaker who was anxious to discover the identity of Mr X and what had happened to Full Back. 'Excuse me for asking,' he asked, 'but who dug that grave? It wasn't Jones, that's for sure. It's almost professional. What's more, who's that toff who threw the earth, not to mention the stones, on the coffin?'

When he had heard all the details, minus any information about Tom Cadwallader's drunken incapacity, he wandered off back to the mourners nearby to tell the story about Full Back's injury. I had told him that Gareth Andrews was standing in for Tom because the grave-digger had 'been taken short'. Mr Matthews was most impressed that the new doctor had volunteered his services. 'Sounds like a good man,' he said.

I went back to the scene of the Cadwallader siesta to find Gareth kneeling alongside the recumbent figure. 'He is still in the arms of Morpheus, I'm afraid. He won't be in any fit state to fill in that grave today. I would suggest that we leave him here for the time being. If you can provide me with a spade, I shall do my best to fill in the grave.' We went back to the boiler-house where the grave-digging implements were kept. He looked at the pick. 'That's a nasty-looking tool,' he said. 'I tell you what, if old Tom had been using it he would have pinned his foot to the floor. It's a good thing that your Full Back is such a half-hearted worker who wouldn't use up much energy in his work. He probably gave it a gentle prod.' He put the spade over his shoulder and began to sing the dwarfs' chorus from Disney's *Snow White*: 'Heigh ho, heigh ho, as off to work we go.'

In no time at all, spadefuls of earth were raining down into the grave. Granny Walters' coffin disappeared very quickly. It took Gareth under an hour to fill in the earth and level it off.

'If ever you lose your job,' I said, 'I'll take you on here for a reasonable wage. Excellent. Thank you very much indeed.' The sweat was streaming down his face and his cravat had been stuffed into his trouser-pocket. His hair was straggling over his forehead. He had tucked his trousers into his socks to prevent any soiling of them, but his once-polished shoes were now bedaubed with top-quality Pontywen mud.

As we went back to the vestry to collect his jacket, we were met by Eleanor and Heather who showed the same reaction as the undertaker and the mourners at the sight of Gareth. 'What on earth have you been doing?' demanded Heather. 'Look at the state of you!'

'It's my fault,' I said.

'I might have known,' remarked my wife.

'No, it's not his fault at all,' Gareth interrupted her as she was about to elaborate on various incidents in my past. 'I volunteered to fill in a grave.' The two girls stared at him as if he had taken leave of his senses.

'I should have said it's our fault, love,' I explained. 'Tom Cadwallader is lying behind a gravestone, paralytically inebriate. Since we supplied him with the means to achieve that state and it was you who suggested we give him beer with his fish and chips, I suppose it is our fault.' The explanation was followed by a stunned silence. 'I think more to the point at the moment, is how we are to bring him back from the Land of Nod and how I am going to explain to Mrs Cadwallader, pillar of the Mothers' Union in Llanhyfryd, that the vicar rendered her husband drunk and incapable.'

'The first thing is to get him to the vicarage and fill him with black coffee,' said Eleanor. 'Let me get my jacket from the vestry first,' suggested Gareth, 'then Fred and I can pick him up between us and propel him in the direction of the vicarage.'

'In that case,' my wife replied, 'Heather and I will get back there as quickly as possible and get the coffee brewing.'

By the time Gareth and I returned to the gravestone behind which Tom Cadwallader had collapsed into inertia, there were signs that the giant was coming back to life. His snoring had ceased and his attitude of careless abandon had given way to a knees-up position with his back against the stone.

'Are you awake, Tom?' I shouted. He shook his head as if the noise of my voice was more than he could bear. A frown wrinkled his smooth forehead and one eye opened in an attempt to focus on me.

'Vicar,' he murmured, 'where am I?'

'You're in the churchyard, Tom, and we are going to help you up and get you back to the vicarage. Then we shall take you home to Llanhyfryd.'

Slowly, very slowly, his senses returned. 'What about the funeral, Vicar? Have they come yet?'

'They have come and gone. Now we want you to come with us.'

Gareth looked over the grave-digger's head at me and winked. 'Now then, old man,' he said, 'we are going to put our arms around you to help you up. One, two, three.' It was like trying to lift a recalcitrant elephant. Any more attempts like that and I was in danger of incurring a hernia.

'What about the grave?' slurred Tom.

'Don't worry about that. This gentleman has filled it in.'

He stared at Gareth. 'He has?'

'Yes, it has all been seen to.' Tom shook his head slowly in disbelief. He still showed no inclination to leave his tombstone.

'Come on, Tom. Mrs Cadwallader will be wondering where you have got to.'

The mention of his wife's name acted like an alarm-bell. He swivelled his bottom around and used his long arms to catch hold of the stone to haul himself up. He remained draped over the memorial to Thomas Arthur Davies and his family for a minute or two.

I began to wonder if the bulk of his weight would make the gravestone keel over. 'Ready to move now?' I inquired. 'We'll come on either side of you to steady you.'

He left his anchorage and attempted to stand. It was fortunate that he listed towards Gareth who was strong enough to withstand the pressure. Had it been towards me, we would have been in a heap, with myself the flattened middle of a sandwich between Tom and Pontywen Churchyard.

Slowly our trio began to move towards the vicarage like a human inchworm. By the time we reached the church gates, Tom's head was beginning to clear and his legs showed a degree of co-ordination. As we came down the vicarage drive, we had an interested audience watching us through the sitting-room window.

Eleanor and Heather came out to meet us, showing unseemly signs of merriment to the extent of wiping tears from their eyes. 'Come round the side to the kitchen,' said Eleanor. 'I've got a jug of black coffee ready.'

Once inside the kitchen, Tom slumped into a chair. 'Here you are, Tom, a mug of nice black coffee. That will put you right in no time.' She placed the mug firmly into his hands.

'Don't drink coffee,' he said.

'You try this coffee. It's a special brand. You'll love it,' coaxed my wife.

He put the receptacle to his mouth and took a deep gulp. Then he shuddered. It reminded me of the way my father drank whisky – a shudder with every mouthful. Tom wiped his hand across his mouth and took another large swallow, then another. He finished the jug of coffee as quickly as he had consumed the beer earlier.

'Better get back,' he announced, and stood up as steadily as if he had never been in contact with the demon drink. I heaved a sigh of relief.

When we arrived at his cottage, Mrs Cadwallader was at the gate, in a state of high dudgeon. 'I thought you would have been back long before now, Vicar. His dinner has dried up in the oven.'

'For a number of reasons, it took longer than I thought, I'm afraid. Anyway, I have paid Tom overtime, as it were. So he got two pounds ten instead of two pounds. I hope that will compensate for the inconvenience.'

This news had its desired effect. The scowl vanished from Mrs Cadwallader's face and her beloved was welcomed, not with open arms, but with considerably less hostility than otherwise.

That night, when Gareth and Heather had gone, my wife and I were relaxing in the sitting-room before retiring. 'Well, love,' she said. 'Granny Walters is up there, absolutely delighted. She has been lying in state in the Parish church, surrounded by flowers provided by the mayor and corporation. It has taken two grave-diggers to dig her grave, but the final accolade is the best of all, the grave has been filled in by the new doctor in Pontywen. Her cup must be running over.'

9

The clouds were queueing up to empty themselves on Pontywen the next morning, after a week of unbroken sunshine. 'Do you think the Almighty is trying to tell Dai Spout something, as a non-attending Baptist who switched his allegiance to the Church for the sake of prestige? Then there is his wife, a non-attending Anglican who has seen to it that her objectionable young son has been confirmed in order to give weight to his testimonial when he applies for a job. What a pair! No wonder a deep depression has rushed in from the west.' Eleanor was looking out through our bedroom window on a typical rainswept Valley scene.

'He sendeth the rain on the just and the unjust, according to the Sermon on the Mount,' I replied, 'and like it or not, I am the mayor's chaplain for the next twelve months, so we had better make the most of it.'

'Come on, Frederick, where's your sense of humour? You sound just as pompous as Dai Spout himself. If being mayor's chaplain has this effect on you, you'll be unbearable by this time next year. When you say, we had better make the most of it, surely that means we can have plenty of laughs out of the experience.'

'OK, love. You win. Perhaps I am treating the whole business too seriously. What about rejoining the Gilbert and Sullivan Society? After all, you now have a partner in your practice. So your workload will be much lighter and Aneurin still has not found a leading soprano. It means, too, that I shall have to persuade Iorweth Ellis that he is at his best as a chorus-leader. Then I can take over the tenor lead again and play Marco to your Gianetta.'

'You Machiavellian vicar, you! Then, of course, you will tell Aneurin not to bother about asking his colleague to take over the production and you will be in full charge once again. You are not only Machiavellian, you are Pooh Bah as well.'

'I acknowledge my transgressions and my pride is ever before me. Yes, you are dead right. I should love to take over the production once again. It will certainly be a busy time but the G & S will be the perfect antidote to a year with Mr and Mrs Dai Spout. With the help of *The Gondoliers* I shall be able to survive.'

'With the help of a quick bath and shave, you will be able to take the eight o'clock service. You had better get a move on, love. The godly few will have an unforgettable experience awaiting them, a quiet communion with the Almighty in Kew Gardens. They will not appreciate a breathless arrival of the vicar into their midst, I can assure you.'

It was ten to eight when I slipped into the vestry by the side door to be greeted by David Vaughan-Jenkins, the vicar's warden, who made a point of being in the church for the early communion at least a quarter of an hour before the service was due to commence. 'Very impressive, Vicar,' he said. 'I have never seen the church look so lovely, though I must confess I should have preferred a colour scheme of blue and white rather than red and yellow. Still, beggars can't be choosers.' He had once been an unsuccessful Conservative candidate in a by-election in the Valleys, with a five per cent share of the vote. 'I still bear the scars,' he had told me.

'Everything is ready, Vicar,' said Gwyn Evans as he came into the vestry from the sanctuary. He was a pleasant sixteen-year-old who acted as server at that service and who was as punctual as the churchwarden. 'The place is ponging like a – a lady's boudoir. I nearly fell over a pot of geraniums when I was putting out the bread and wine.' He grinned like a Cheshire cat and proceeded to put on his surplice to hide his blushes.

I went out into the heavily scented air of the chancel, accompanied by the server, to commence the service for the regular dozen who attended because they did not wish to be distracted by the singing and the sermon which were an essential part of the eleven o'clock Eucharist, twelve individuals who each had their private line to the source of their being.

All was proceeding according to the usual pattern of this service until it reached the administration of the bread and wine. One by one the worshippers came out of their pews slowly as if loath to reach the altar rails. Then it happened. Miss Doris Williams, an elderly spinster, a devout lady with a large nose and spectacles which seemed to have difficulty in surmounting it, collapsed as the queue was forming in the chancel. I was standing with a wafer poised between my thumb and forefinger when the worshippers formed a scrum around the unconscious Miss Williams who had been caught in his arms by David Vaughan-Jenkins as she fell.

Since Doris Williams was scarcely more than six or seven stone in weight, the churchwarden was able to carry her into the vestry as if she were a babe-in-arms. As they disappeared the rest of the worshippers recovered their composure and the service continued. When I had given the blessing, Gwyn and I proceeded into the vestry to find Miss Williams sitting up in my chair with a complexion like a whited sepulchre. 'I'm so sorry, Vicar,' she breathed. 'I must have fainted. I always fast before my communion, as you know. It may be that the strong scent of those lovely flowers affected my empty stomach. I have never passed out like this before. It was providential that Mr Vaughan-Jenkins was behind me to catch me as I fell.' She gave him one of her special smiles. He reciprocated with a faint glimpse of his teeth.

As he counted the collection, he informed her that he would take her home in his car once his duties in church were over. He was rewarded with one of her extra-special smiles.

When they had gone, Gwyn said to me as he was leaving, 'It's a good thing Mrs Vaughan-Jenkins wasn't here. Otherwise he'd be in trouble, wouldn't he?'

'Go on home, you naughty boy,' I told him. 'Otherwise you will be in trouble.'

'How did the eight o'clock contingent like the decorations?' inquired Eleanor when I returned to the vicarage.

'At least one of them regarded it as a knock-out,' I replied. 'Miss Williams, Sebastopol Street, fainted as she approached the altar rails and blamed it on the strong scent of the flowers. She left me stranded with the wafer in my hand while everybody else turned their attention on her. However, David, the warden, caught her as she fell and carried her into the vestry.'

'That must be the one and only romantic moment in her life,' said my wife. 'I should not be surprised if she contrives one or two more collapses if David happens to be behind her in the godly queue.'

'You're as bad as young Gwyn Evans, Eleanor. He suggested that the warden would have been in trouble if his wife had been there.'

'I don't think Elvira Vaughan-Jenkins, president of the WI and valued customer of Pontywen's only ladies' hairdressing salon would consider Doris Williams a rival for her husband's affections. She would be much more concerned if her husband's head was turned by some of the ladies who will be present at the social event of the year this afternoon.'

'It is not a social event, love. It is just a civic service. The mayor-making was the social event, not a wet afternoon in St Mary's.'

'As far as Elvira is concerned, this afternoon is what matters. She was not invited to the mayor-making. So today's service will be her only contact with the VIPs of the borough. I can guarantee you will find her hovering around the back of the church as the distinguished company arrives ready to impress in a new outfit which cost a bomb and most of her clothing coupons.'

She was right, as usual. When I entered the church through the drenching rain, the first person I met in the porch was Mrs Vaughan-Jenkins who was standing in the open doorway, arrayed in an expensively cut two-piece and looking like the lady of the manor waiting to receive her guests at a dinner-party.

'What a terrible day, Vicar,' she breathed. 'Isn't the church looking lovely? Such a profusion of flowers. A little gaudy, perhaps, and such a preponderance of red and yellow. The mayoress's choice, I gather. It's a good thing I am wearing pea-green. It will help to reduce the monotony of colour. David insisted on coming early to supervise everything, so of course I had to come with him. I thought I might while away the time making our visitors feel at home while the men are giving out the service leaflets, etcetera. A woman's touch is always helpful, isn't it, Vicar?'

'It all depends on the time and the place, I suppose, Mrs Vaughan-Jenkins. I expect your husband will be glad of your help.' So saying, I moved on into the church where David was giving instructions to Idris the Milk and Charlie Hughes about their part in the proceedings. Harold Jones, the people's warden, was placing 'reserved' cards in the front pew to the accompaniment of Mr Greenfield at the organ where he was attempting to play Jeremiah Clark's 'Trumpet Voluntary'. The air was filled with the overpowering scent of the floral decorations to such an extent that any member of the congregation who suffered from hay fever would not be able to survive the service without severe damage to the nasal passages.

Half an hour later, the church was full of chattering guests and the porch was full of steaming mackintoshes. The mayoral party had not arrived, with only five minutes left before the service was due to commence. In the vestry there was an excited hubbub as members of St Padarn's choir who had been invited to augment the parish church contingent were being placed in line for the ceremonial procession into the nave by Mr Greenfield prior to his rapid departure to the organ stool for Jeremiah Clark's masterpiece.

'Now, calm down, everybody,' I shouted. The noise diminished. 'Remember where you are. This is God's house, not Pontywen Square on a Saturday. It's OK, Mr Greenfield, you had better get back to the organ now.'

He turned to go out and was almost bowled over by Bertie Owen coming post-haste into the vestry.

'The mayor's car is blocked by some cars outside the church, Vicar.'

'Aren't the wardens seeing to that, Bertie?'

'Yes, they're out there getting soaking wet, but I thought you ought to know.'

'Did they ask you to come and tell me?'

'Not exactly.'

'I am sure they did not. They have arranged for some-one to come and tell me when the mayor is in the church porch. Why do you have to poke your nose in, Bertie? Would you mind joining the congregation while I wait for the message that the mayor and mayoress have arrived.'

This conversation was heard with great amusement by the choir as if it were a double act in a music hall. A minute or two later Harold Jones came to inform me that the mayoral party were in the porch. 'They are very upset at being obstructed by the cars outside, Vicar, so that they couldn't park outside the church doors. We got umbrellas to shelter them but you know what the wind is like. I'm afraid they're a bit wet.'

They were very upset indeed by the time I had gone to

the door to receive them and lead them down the aisle. The mayoress was distraught. 'Look at my hair,' she moaned, 'let alone my new suit. Everything is going wrong. First of all, you pulled the curtain down on us at the reception. Then you had somebody dead in here when they were doing the flowers and now this.'

'I am very sorry, Mayoress. I may have pulled the curtain down on you but I am not responsible for the rain.'

'But you are responsible for keeping a space outside the door for us, Vicar.' said the mayor. 'It's an understood thing, as it were. Anyway, let's get on with it.' I gave the signal to Mr Greenfield to begin the 'Trumpet Voluntary'.

We moved down the aisle to the tentative rendering of the ceremonial music as the congregation stood to receive the chief citizens of the borough and their entourage. After I had ushered them into their places, I went to the vestry to say the opening prayer with the choir before they moved into the church. When I opened the door, I was greeted by a noise several decibels greater than before. I closed the door with a bang. 'Quiet,' I yelled. There was a deathly hush. 'It's a good thing Mr Greenfield has all the stops out on the organ, otherwise all the council would have heard the commotion here. Let's have good behaviour in church as well as good singing. Now, let us pray.'

As a safety precaution, I had made sure Charles was not involved in the service by asking him to take charge of a joint Sunday school in the parish hall that afternoon. I had not bargained for the mayor's contribution to the service. He had been asked to read the second lesson, St Paul's Epistle to the Romans – Chapter 13, verse 10 to the end. Dai Spout came to the lectern after the hymn had finished. I had tried to catch his attention during the singing to alert him. He buried his face in the hymn-book, making any visual signal to him impossible. Fortunately the pages had been made ready for him by Ezekiel Evans who had read the first lesson complete with dropped aitches and a full quota of misplaced ones.

The mayor adjusted his spectacles and cleared his throat. He read slowly, with a faint touch of the Welsh *hwyl* in his voice. When he came to the end of the chapter, I stood up to begin the next part of the service. To my consternation, he carried on reading the next chapter. By the time he came to verse 6 – 'He that eateth, eateth to the Lord, for he giveth God thanks and he that eateth not to the Lord, to the Lord he eateth not' – I decided to end the suffering of a bemused congregation. I came out from my stall and tapped him on the shoulder. He reacted like a startled fawn.

'The lesson should have finished at the end of the chapter,' I whispered.

'I'm sorry, Vicar, I thought it meant that I had to read on to the end of the Epistle.' Since that would have entailed another three chapters, it was obvious that he was prepared to stay at the lectern for most of the afternoon. He was not nicknamed Dai Spout for nothing. As he returned to his pew he was greeted by a glare from his spouse. In stark contrast was the sense of relief evident on the faces of the congregation.

I began my sermon with the words,'My text is taken from the lesson read so ably by the mayor, "Let us walk honestly as in the day."' The chief citizen smirked with self-satisfaction. It was a smirk which disappeared as the sermon developed.

'The keystone of local government must be honesty. Everything out in the open. Walk honestly as in the day, not skulk under the cover of night. There must be no deals behind closed doors. There must be no place for bribes to secure headships or to gain lucrative contracts for building firms. When citizens pay their taxes they expect their money to be used in fair administration, not to line the packets of a few.'

It was one of those rare occasions when it could be said that the silence was such that you could hear a pin drop. 'I am speaking generally, of course,' I went on. 'I am sure that in this borough there is the probity of honest men who have been elected to serve their fellow citizens. To be a councillor involves a great deal of self-sacrifice, the loss of one's spare time and putting up with innumerable inconveniences. In other words it is only the dedicated who can accept the challenge of being a councillor. They have come to church today because they need our prayers as much as they need your votes. Above all we pray today for your new mayor. May he walk tall and honestly as in the day and may his lady mayoress be enabled to be his mainstay throughout the next twelve months.'

As I passed the front pew on my way to the sanctuary, from the corner of my eye I could see six frowning faces engaged in singing 'O happy band of pilgrims', in a tight-lipped rendition which boded ill for the farewell at the end of the service. When I had given the blessing, I proceeded down the chancel to the front pew to escort them down the aisle. I felt as if I were leading a party of mourners at the funeral of a loved one. When we reached the porch I turned to shake hands with them. 'Look!' I said, 'The sun is coming out.'

'That is the only bright spot of the afternoon,' growled the mayor. 'What did you mean by raking up all those old lies about corruption in the Council? The pulpit isn't the place for that kind of thing, as it were.'

'Neither is the church porch the place to start a discussion on the matter, Mr Mayor,' I replied. 'I did not accuse any councillor in this borough of such behaviour. I was speaking generally, as I pointed out. Perhaps we could have a talk about this at a more convenient time and place.'

'We'll do nothing of the sort, Vicar. I appointed you to be my chaplain, not my political adviser, as it were,' he said. 'My husband is quite right,' added the mayoress. 'I'm sorry in my heart now that I ever pushed him into asking you to be his chaplain. It's been a proper disaster, that's all I can say. We'd better be going, Dai.'

They went without a handshake, as did most of the councillors, who seemed to be in a hurry to escape. However, there were members of the congregation only too eager to shake my hand and congratulate me on saying something which ought to have been said publicly long ago. When they had all gone, David Vaughan-Jenkins was fulsome in his praise of the sermon. 'As an ex-Conservative candidate in this constituency, I think you did a great job in the pulpit today. I could tell you of many cases of bribery and corruption, but as a bank manager my lips are sealed. What you did took courage, young man.'

'Perhaps it was foolhardiness rather than courage,' I replied. 'Judging by the reception I had from the council members as they left the church, it would appear that I have blotted my copy book. I have a shrewd suspicion that I shall not be invited to many functions in this mayoral year.'

'Well, I do not think you will have missed much,' suggested Elvira who had come to join us. 'Did you see some of those outfits? Those councillors' wives have as much dress sense as the gypsies on Pontywen Common, I don't know why I bothered to get a new outfit for the occasion. I thought at least there would be some of the more important people of the borough present like the captains of industry and their wives. You would have thought that at least Sir David Jones-Williams and Lady Jones-Williams would have been invited, for example. As it was, it was more like a Trades Union outing.'

'I must admit, Mrs Vaughan-Jenkins, I did not expect a fashion display this afternoon, unlike my wife who thought, as you did, that there would be an element of high society mingling with the riff-raff. Perhaps the mayor was influenced by his wife in his selection of invited guests, in case she suffered from competition. In any case, as far as I am concerned I am sure there is corruption in high-society circles and if I had to preach to a convention of captains of industry, as you call them, I would preach the same sermon.'

When I went back to the vicarage, my wife greeted me with open arms. 'Well done, you lovely man! That was a sermon straight from the shoulder, as they say. You should have seen Dai Spout's face and that of his missus, if it comes to that, as they followed you down the aisle at the end of the service. I tell you one thing, they will never forgive you for that.'

'You are quite right, my love. I received a ticking-off after which they departed without shaking hands. Dear Elvira applauded my effort afterwards but for the wrong reasons. She thought I was putting the lower orders in their place and bewailed the absence of the captains of industry and their wives among the guests. I told her that if I had been preaching to the said captains I would have preached the same sermon on the assumption that there was just as much corruption amongst them as there is in the Council Chamber.'

'Frederick, you really are developing into a firebrand. I tell you something, you will be making headline news in the local paper. I saw a reporter there this afternoon. He was scribbling like mad when you came to the juicier part of your sermon. You may have started a first-class row. I bet the correspondence column will be full of letters on the subject.'

Next morning, after Matins, Charles was eager to hear more about the sermon. 'Idris the Milk said it was one of the best sermons he had ever heard and that Dai Spout looked absolutely murderous as he left the church. They were all talking about it at evensong. Even Mrs Collier said it was good.'

'Look, Charles, I have preached much better sermons than that, I hope. They are only making such a fuss about it because I chanced to say something which everybody talks about privately but never in public. I thought that yesterday's service was the occasion to bring out the matter of local government bribery and corruption into the open. I felt strongly about it after hearing one or two things after the mayor-making ceremony. Anyway, let's forget all about it. I am more concerned today to find out how Eleanor's new partner is doing in his debut at the surgery. She is keeping her fingers crossed that she has picked a winner. If she has, it will make life a lot easier for her.'

When she came home at lunchtime, she had a large smile on her face. 'What a difference!' she exclaimed.

'Normally on a Monday morning the waiting-room is still full at eleven o'clock. Today by eleven there wasn't a sound of a cough or a sight of a patient. It was gloriously empty. Not only that, but according to the dragon, when the patients came out of Gareth Andrews' room they were all more than satisfied with their treatment.'

The dragon was Miss Philpott, the receptionist, who had been in the surgery since before Eleanor was born. Even if the patients were satisfied with the new doctor it would be a long time before she gave her approval.

'What's more, he was very keen to do his share of house visits after surgery,' Eleanor said. 'He said he wanted to find his way about Pontywen as soon as possible. I feel as if a tremendous weight has been lifted off my shoulders. We should be able to have that holiday we have promised ourselves for so long. Cornwall, here we come.' She caught hold of me and gave me a bear-hug.

'I tell you what, my love,' I breathed, 'now that tremendous weight has been lifted off your shoulders they aren't half strong.'

That afternoon I had to attend the quarterly meeting of the deanery clergy in the back room of the Bull Inn at Tremadoc. There was the usual quota of ancient clerics sunk into the armchairs and the two settees. It was my turn to read a chapter of the chosen study book, *The Minor Prophets in the Twentieth Century*.

The minutes were read by the drawling Obadiah Morris, the chapter clerk, whose voice had such a soporific effect that by the time he had finished, not only was the Reverend Thomas Hughes, Rector of Llansantffraidd with Pentwyn, aged eighty-six years and the Rip Van Winkle of the deanery, sound asleep, but at least three others were looking at me through half-lidded eyes. It was not an encouraging sight for any speaker.

I thought I would enliven the proceedings by telling a weak joke I had been told about Malachi, the last of the minor prophets, the subject of the chapter. 'A long-winded preacher had been boring his congregation with a complete tour through the books of the minor Prophets. "And now," he said, "we come at last to Malachi: 'Where shall we put Malachi?'" The squire, who had been sitting in the front pew, sat up. "You can put him here," he said, "I have had enough," and stalked out.'

Far from enlivening the proceedings, I found I had succeeded in closing the three pairs of half-lidded eyes completely. I was left with the rural dean, the chapter clerk and the Reverend Williams-Evans, the deanery's liaison officer with the religious bookshop in Cardiff. By the time I had dealt with the argument for a possible date of authorship as 460 BC or even a later date nearer 315 BC, their eyes had again reached the half-lidded state. I read through the rest of the chapter as loudly and as quickly as I could to prevent being the only one awake in a comatose gathering. Valiantly, those three pairs of half-closed eyes had striven to keep the lids apart. As I finished, the rural dean stretched himself in his armchair and with his arms extended above his head, announced, 'Now then, let's have some tea.' The word 'tea' was sufficient to rouse two of the sleepers but not to wake Rip Van Winkle, who was still in the Land of Nod when I left.

As I drove back to Pontywen I wondered if my sermon had made the headlines in the evening paper. When my car pulled up outside the vicarage door, I was greeted by an excited Eleanor waving the early edition of the

Monmouthshire Post. I jumped out of the car and ran up the steps. 'You have reached stardom, Frederick – the front page of the paper, with a photograph of you taken on the day of your induction. I tell you what, it is the first time a parson's words have taken precedence over those of the local MP or the Trades Union bosses, not to mention the captains of industry.'

She handed me the newspaper. There on the front page was emblazoned in big block capitals, 'MAYOR'S CHAPLAIN ATTACKS TOWN HALL CORRUPTION'. Underneath was a verbatim report of my sermon, but omitting the words 'I am speaking generally' and giving the impression that I was referring to my own borough. 'That, my love,' said my wife, 'will really put the cat amongst the pigeons.'

It was not long before there was a considerable fluttering in the dovecote. Inevitably the first sign of panic came from the mayor. He was on the telephone before we sat down for our evening meal. It was no exaggeration to say that for a man noted for his flow of words he was extremely incoherent. From what I could gather he was telling me that I had opened a whole can of worms and that God knows where they were going to crawl, as it were. Furthermore he suggested that if I wanted to be a politician I should use a soap-box not a pulpit.

Not long afterwards the town clerk rang up to say that my insinuations would have to be substantiated and if not there would be grave legal consequences for me. He was followed by the leader of the council, noted for his itching palm. He was trying desperately to find if I had any substance for my accusations and sounded very relieved to know that I had not.

'Perhaps now we can have some peace for our dinner,'

said my wife, when I had put the phone down. 'It is a surprise treat to celebrate the new partnership. Mrs Thomas, Cwmdulais Farm, gave us that trout when I was there earlier this afternoon – a thank-you for easing her arthritis.'

As she said this, the telephone rang yet again. 'The Vicar of Pontywen speaking,' I said.

'This is the *Daily Mail* here,' the voice replied.

10

'For heaven's sake, Iorwerth, try to *look* happy when you sing "We're happy as happy can be" and, by the way, tripping to the right does not mean giving an imitation of a cart horse.'

Iorwerth Ellis, tenor, with aspirations to take the tenor lead, looked at me with a decidedly sour expression on his face. When some months previously I had signified my intention of opting out of the production of *The Gondoliers*, he had been convinced that stardom had arrived for him, despite his complete lack of any histrionic ability. Now that I had come back as tenor lead and producer, he had to be content with the minor role of Antonio with one small solo and no lines to speak. His cup of bitterness was overflowing.

It was now four months since the civic service. My sermon had been a nine days' wonder, but not in the mind of the mayor who confined my duties to the saying of prayers at the monthly council meetings. This meant that I was free to indulge my passion for Gilbert and Sullivan, and to play opposite Eleanor whose burden of work had been made so much lighter now that she had an excellent partner in her practice. Gereth and Heather had married and were living in Ashburnam Close, the elite cul-de-sac in Pontywen.

One of the fringe benefits of the marriage was Heather's mezzo soprano voice and her amateur stage experience. She was given the part of Tessa, joining

Eleanor's Gianetta in an attractive blonde and brunette combination. The only fringe benefit from my chaplaincy was the advent of Rhoda Powell, the parks superintendent's wife. She was an Amazon with a powerful contralto voice perfectly suited to the Duchess of Plaza Toro, whose consort was a little weed of a man, Trevor Willis, a comic actor *par excellence*.

Bronwen's pregnancy was at the visible stage and she had given up her nursing at the hospital. This meant that Charles was always on time at Matins, with a wife to push him out of bed. She had undertaken to come and help Gwen Shoemaker, wife of Idris the Milk, in making tea for the cast during the break in rehearsal and giving moral support to her husband at the piano.

The musical director, Aneurin Williams, teacher of music at Pontywen Grammar School, provided the female chorus from his senior pupils and this year had recruited some of the young men from the Sixth Form, including Malcolm Evans, the head prefect, whose young tenor voice and appearance made him a natural for the role of Luiz, the Duke's attendant. As Aneurin said, after one rehearsal, 'You are lucky, Vicar, to have so much youth in your chorus. It is a refreshing change from the other societies in the Valleys whose female complement would be better employed at home knitting matinee coats for their grandchildren.'

We were still rehearsing in St Padarn's Church, a corrugated iron edifice, with the pews and chairs pushed to one side to make a playing arena, and chalk marks indicating the size of the stage in the Grammar School hall where the production would take place. After an hour of strenuous chorus exertion involved in the opening of *The Gondoliers*, I called a halt for the tea-break.

Heather, Eleanor and myself were joined by Gareth who was paying his first visit to the Society. 'I must say I am most impressed by your chorus, especially the girls. They are obviously quite young but blessed with good voices as well as good looks. Where did you find them?'

'He did not find them,' said my wife. 'They are almost all of them pupils of the musical director, as I was myself once. It was fortunate for my husband that he married someone who recruited his MD, who in turn recruited his chorus. I am beginning to wonder if that was the reason why he married me.'

Before I could reply the church door was flung open and the burly figure of Will Book and Pencil strode towards us. 'Excuse me for interrupting, but it is an emergency. There has been a roof fall down at the pit. I tried to get you at the vicarage. Then I went to Ezekiel Evans and he said you were here. I didn't think you were here as well, Dr Andrews. That's what you call prudential, isn't it?'

In no time at all, Eleanor and Gareth had driven to the surgery in his car to pick up their Gladstone bags, leaving behind alarm, where only minutes previously there had been happiness and excitement at the first stage rehearsal.

'Charlie Thomas and Harry Williams are on the two-till-ten shift,' said Bertie Owen. 'That's why they had to miss tonight's practice.'

'My father's on that shift too,' added Malcolm Evans.

'And mine,' said two of the girls.

'There's no point in carrying on tonight,' I announced. 'Perhaps it is not as bad as it sounds and no one has been badly injured. In any case the three of you had better get home as quickly as possible. Your mothers will need all the support you can give them at a time like this. See you all next Thursday when I hope all things will be back to normal and nothing drastic has happened.'

The three young people hurried out into the October night while the rest of the cast began to leave in a hubbub of concern and speculation. 'Will they have to go underground?' asked Heather in tones of great perturbation.

'I don't know whether they both will have to do that. Perhaps one will have to stay at the pit-head to tend to the men who have been brought up in an injured condition. It all depends on what has happened, how bad a fall it is and how many are trapped.'

'Can I be of any use?' inquired Bronwen. 'I should think a trained nurse would be of great help at the pit-head.'

'You're not going down there,' ordered Charles. 'You've got our child to think of and in any case by now they will have alerted the hospital. So there should be plenty of trained nurses available.'

'You can never have enough trained nurses if it is a really big accident,' persisted his wife.

'I tell you what,' I said, 'let's all go down there, the four of us, and see what is involved. I am sure that I will be needed as a priest and so will you, Charles, if there is anything of a serious nature. So let's go round to the vicarage and pick up the car. Then we can see for ourselves what is needed.'

As we walked to the vicarage, we could hear the warning bell of an ambulance on its way to the colliery. There was a sense of menace in the air as the sound of one bell died away and another distant bell broke the brief silence. Conversation was minimal. Our minds were too full of foreboding to speculate on the extent of the accident. Pontywen Colliery had always had a good safety record. Apart from the occasional death of an individual, there had never been a major incident, but this one boded ill.

It seemed that every street through which we drove was fearful of what had happened under the ground on which the terraces were built. Little knots of people were gathered around open doorways. All the euphoria which had come from the nationalization of the mines on 1 January 1947 was evaporating with the realization two years later that coal not only provided the community's way of life but paid for it at the cost of human sacrifice.

When we reached the colliery, there was a large crowd of anxious relatives outside, waiting for news of their loved ones. The constables stood in front of the closed gates. I parked the car further up the street. 'Stay here,' I said to my passengers, 'I'll have a word with the police to find out what the situation is and to see whether we'll be needed inside the gates.'

One of the constables recognized me at first sight. 'Hello, Vicar. Nasty business, isn't it? Eight of them trapped by the fall. Most of the shift had gone on ahead, fortunately, when the roof collapsed on their mates behind them. They are down there helping but it must have been an extensive fall. I should think there'll be quite a few dead and a lot of casualties.'

'Can I be of any use?' I asked. 'I have my curate with me and his wife who is a trained nurse. My wife is a doctor and she is already here with her partner.'

'I think the best thing is if you will go inside and find out. I know Dr Secombe is here. She and the other doctor were the first on the scene. They are underground, as far as I know. Anyway, go and see for yourself what is needed of you. Go to the manager's office, they'll be able to tell you.'

After I had run back to the car to keep the others informed, I made my way to the manager's office, following the directions given me by the constable. As I did so, I could see stretchers being unloaded into a fleet of waiting ambulances. Inside the office there was total confusion, the telephone was ringing constantly, clerks were running about, colliding with each other in the process. A police superintendent was engaged in earnest conversation with the manager, Haydn Price Williams, a former rugby international. As I hovered in their vicinity, I caught the eye of Mr Price Williams. 'Can I help in any way,' I asked, 'underground or at the pit-head?'

'They won't want you underground, you would be in the way. You could be of help when the injured come up by offering comfort of some kind. At the moment, the less cluttering up there is the better.' If the situation at the pit-head was as chaotic as that in the office, I could see his point.

I decided that I had better get back to the car first to let my passengers know that they were surplus to requirement. Charles was much relieved but Heather was worried about her husband being underground. 'How do you think I feel about Eleanor?' I told her. 'The best thing you can do, the three of you, is to get back home. As soon as I know anything about Gareth, I'll let you know.' I gave her the car keys with instructions to drive the Wentworth-Baxters' home and to leave my car at her place in Ashburnam Close until I phoned her with further news.

By the time I reached the pit-head, there were a half-dozen ambulances queuing up to ferry the injured to hospital. As I rushed towards the pit-shaft, I strained my eyes to see if there was any sign of my wife, but to no avail. Then I recognized a nurse from Pontywen Hospital who was about to get into an ambulance with one of the stretcher cases. The miner lay with his eyes closed, sweat dribbling white streaks on the black canvas of his face. As the two stretcher-bearers lifted him carefully into the vehicle, I suddenly realized it was Charlie Thomas, one of the Gilbert and Sullivan chorus who was on that shift. 'Charlie,' I shouted.

He opened his eyes and focused on me. 'I tell you what, Vicar, your missus is doing wonders down there. See you soon.' Then he went back into oblivion.

'I doubt it,' said the nurse, 'but what he said is true. They say that Dr Secombe and Dr Andrews have both been crawling through the debris to inject the trapped men with painkillers to ease them, apart from seeing to those who have been injured on the other side of the fall.'

Ambulances came and went with the dead and injured. The hours went by and the pit-cages came up with tired rescuers, but there was still no sign of Eleanor and Gareth. Then, to my intense relief, two doctors from the Casualty Department at Pontywen Hospital arrived. They told me that they had come to take over from Eleanor and Gareth. By now the overpowering smell of coal dust was clogging my lungs and biting into my soul. I wondered how men could endure such afflictions to earn a living, even if they had rid themselves of the coal owners who had exploited them over the past 160 years or so. I had tried to comfort the injured as they arrived at the surface. It was a pointless exercise. They had looked death in the face. All I had to offer came from a life untroubled by constant physical danger and cocooned in a clerical collar.

I shall never forget the moment when the pit-cage rattled to the top and a little figure in coal-blackened overalls with a miner's helmet on her head emerged amongst another contingent of rescuers. I ran to meet her and picked her up, hugging her as if she were a long-lost relative. 'If I were you, my love,' she said, 'I would put me down unless you want a veneer of anthracite on your best clerical suit. Not only that, but my bones are aching and they can't stand a bear-hug.'

'Where's Gareth?' I asked. 'Heather is beside herself with worry.'

'He's fine but very tired, like me. He is coming up with the next load of helpers from below. I'll tell you something, Fred, I shall never want to go through anything like that again. How those men can spend their lives on their backs in that narrow claustrophobic environment I shall never know, but I tell you what, they are brave men, believe me. It hasn't hit me yet but it will by tomorrow. You will have to cosset me for a few days, I'm afraid.'

'As many days as you like, love. I suppose you saw Charlie Thomas. I had a word with him when he was put in the ambulance.'

'I'm afraid that poor old Charlie has not long to live. His spine has been crushed. It is a miracle that he is still breathing. He told me that Harry Williams is trapped behind that wall of coal with about eighty others. How on earth they are going to get through to them without causing further falls, I don't know. Apparently there is a danger of a fire-damp explosion as well. Already there must be a dozen men who have been killed outright. It was not a pretty sight, Fred.' She caught hold of my arm tightly. 'I had better get to the changing-room and get this gear off. I must wash my face, too, before the grime gets embedded in my wrinkles. You'd better stay here and wait for Gareth to come up.'

While I waited for her colleague to appear, I wondered what had happened to Malcolm Evans' father and to the fathers of Marilyn Owen and Shirley Jones, the two school-girl members of the chorus. Were they among the dead or the living? I thought of Charlie Thomas puffing on his pipe, giving his famous impression of the *Queen Mary* coming up the channel, and then of his wife, a 'plump and pleasing person' who was so proud that at the age of fifty he was a member of the Gilbert and Sullivan chorus. As I waited, a bus-load of men from Abergwynfi Colliery arrived to supplement the rescue team.

Then once again the pit-cage rattled to the top and among its occupants was the tall figure of Gareth Andrews, his shoulders bent and his head down, as if the weight of the world was bearing down upon his jaunty self. I went across to him as he joined the others on the way to the changing-room. He appeared to have more coal on his face than any of the others. It was a complete mask, more appropriate to Man Friday than the newly arrived Doctor Andrews, recently of the RAMC and the handsome occupant of Room 2 in the Pontywen surgery.

'Gareth,' I said as I drew near to him.

He lifted his head and looked at me out of half-lidded eyes. 'Fred, I am absolutely devastated. I was only in at the last stage of the war, long after the Normandy landings, but I tell you what, I never want to be in another do like this. The suffocating atmosphere, the carnage that coal can create, it has been an eye-opener to me. Your wife has been a revelation too. She has been squeezing through the smallest of gaps to try to reach those who are trapped, to administer medical aid. I take my hat off to her.'

'I join you in that,' I replied. 'Heather will be greatly relieved to know that you are OK. She has taken my car to your place and I've told her that I would phone her once I had news of you. Eleanor has gone to wash and get out of her protective clothing. So perhaps you would phone Heather from here to let her know you're OK and I'll wait for Eleanor and you to give me a lift back to your place. Then I think I had better go to see Charlie Thomas's wife and Harry Williams' wife, too, if it comes to that. It's difficult to know where to begin to carry out my job.'

'If you do that half as well as your wife has done hers, Fred, you can rest content. See you very shortly.' He hurried towards the changing-room. By now it was almost one o'clock in the morning and the crowd outside the gates was bigger than ever, eerily silent. About ten minutes later Gareth and Eleanor met me, and the three of us made our way to Gareth's car, which was parked not far from the gates. He had sold his sports model and had invested in a Triumph saloon which he felt was more in keeping with his GP image.

I sat in the front with him, while Eleanor lounged on the back seat, exhausted by her efforts underground. 'I don't know whether I should go to see Charlie's wife or Harry Williams' wife once I have brought you both to the vicarage, love.'

'You will do neither,' commanded my wife. 'It is far too late to be doing that. Why don't you go first thing in the morning after service? By then things may have sorted themselves out. Perhaps the rescue teams will have got through to Harry and his pals. As far as Charlie is concerned, I should think his wife will be at his bedside in the hospital. You will be of far more use to her once you have had a sleep and come to your senses. It's pointless darting around like a scalded cat this time of the night.'

'She's right,' said Gareth. 'I should think it requires a calm state of mind to comfort the nearest and dearest, to use a hackneyed phrase. Far be it from me to teach his grandmother how to suck eggs, I speak only from a medical point of view. As far as I am concerned I shall be only too glad to hit that pillow and shut out the last four or five hours.'

'Hear, hear!' came my wife's voice from the back of the car. So it was that once we had left Ashburnam Close, we retired for the night.

Neither of us slept well. I woke to discover that the

time was only twenty past two and Eleanor was weeping quietly. I could feel her shoulders shaking as she lay with her back to me. I turned towards her and put my right arm around her. I said nothing but just held her close to me. Gradually the tears ceased and her body relaxed. Two hours later we were both awake again. 'I think I'll make a cup of tea,' I said, 'and while I'm up, I'll ring the colliery to find out what the situation is.'

'They've enough to do, Fred, without us adding to their workload. You go downstairs and make the tea, there's a love. Take a couple of aspirins and bring some for me, please. They'll do instead of sleeping pills.' Soon we were asleep once more.

I had set the alarm for seven o'clock but by six o'clock I was wide awake. Eleanor was still asleep. I put on my dressing-gown and went down to the study to telephone the colliery, only to get the engaged signal. I made myself another cup of tea while I waited to phone again. This time the line was free but I had to wait minutes for a reply. A tired voice announced, 'Pontywen Colliery.'

'This is the Vicar of Pontywen speaking,' I replied. 'Sorry to bother you at a time like this, but could you tell me if you have been able to get through to the trapped miners yet? Some of them are my parishioners.'

'I am afraid not, Vicar. The rescue teams are having to go very carefully in case they cause another fall. They are going to be relieved at seven o'clock by men from the Cwmdulais pit, that's all I can say at the moment.'

My next call was to the hospital to inquire about Charlie Thomas. 'He passed away at four o'clock this morning,' said the ward sister. 'He had been in a lot of pain for the few hours he was alive. All I can say is that it was a merciful release, Vicar. Mrs Thomas was with him when he died. She has taken it very well so far but that's because she is still in a state of shock. I think she will need your help badly when the shock wears off.'

Rosie Thomas was childless and had built her life around Charlie, whereas Harry Williams was blessed with a good wife and a large family. If anything were to happen to Harry there would be any amount of support for Dilys Williams. I lit the fire under the boiler so that Eleanor could have a bath to wash away any traces of the coal dust which had clung to her. I could still smell Pontywen Colliery on her as she lay by my side in bed. There was no doubt that if there was a further fall she would have to be underground once again. For her sake as well as for the trapped men, I prayed fervently that there would be no such happening.

At seven o'clock I went to our bedroom with a cup of tea for Eleanor. She was sitting up in bed staring into space. 'I feel as if I haven't been to bed for weeks,' she said. 'My body is still aching after crawling on my belly. How those men work in a space of three or four feet wide day in day out, I don't know. It's a nightmare existence.'

'I rang the colliery at six o'clock. The men are still trapped behind the fall but a fresh team of rescuers has come. Let's hope they will be able to get through to them. I rang the hospital, too. Poor old Charlie died at four o'clock this morning. Rosie was with him. I'll get along to see her first thing after service. By the way, I have lit the boiler. So you can have a bath and relax before going to surgery. I should have another hour in bed, if I were you, and then enjoy a nice breakfast of bacon and egg, cooked by your favourite chef, once you have had your soak in the bathroom.'

'My favourite chef! I didn't know Mrs Watkins was coming in early this morning. Sorry, love, only kidding. Believe me, I can't tell you how much I want those eighty men to be rescued, if it's only for my sake. I don't think I could face another stint in that hell-hole. I'll take your advice and have that extra hour. So hop it, Frederick, and wake me when the time is up.'

To my amazement, when I went to the church to open up for Matins there were some dozen or so parishioners waiting outside. It was the first time since I had been in Pontywen that there had been a congregation for the early morning service. I announced every Sunday that a daily service would be held at nine o'clock but not a single person had ever turned up. Dilys Williams was there with three of her daughters. Even young Malcolm Evans was present. It was only recently that he had begun to attend church after joining the Gilbert and Sullivan Society.

As we robed in the vestry, Charles expressed his great surprise on finding parishioners joining us for our normal duologue. 'This always happens where there is big trouble, I suppose. I remember people turning up in our parish church at home for the National Day of Prayer when the last war was looming. They had never put their foot inside there before nor did they afterwards – it's just one big cry for help, Charles.'

During the service we spent a few minutes in silent prayer for the trapped men. The rest of the service meant little to the worshippers, who knew nothing about Jehosaphat's war with Ahab or the intricate arguments of a chapter in St Paul's Epistle to the Romans. They were in church for one reason only, and in that silence there was an intensity of supplication that no words could express.

I encountered a different kind of silence a little later that morning. When the service was over I made my way to Balaclava Street to see Rosie Thomas. I could feel my heart beating faster, and my throat was dry. How am I going to comfort someone, the centre of whose life has been taken away in an instant? I said to myself. I dreaded facing her in her misery. I stood outside number eleven for quite a while before I could summon up enough courage to knock on the door. It was opened by Gwen Shoemaker. 'Come on in, Vicar,' she whispered. 'We'd better go into the front room for a minute. She's sitting in the kitchen by the fire. The shock has made her feel cold.'

We went into the little parlour. The blinds were drawn but the morning sunshine filtered through sufficiently to illuminate the room without Gwen having to switch on the light. 'Her sister is coming down from Coventry this afternoon. Her husband went up from here to look for work in the depression. He's got a good job now with the car firm. Own house and phone and that sort of thing. So I was able to go to the phone box and ring them for her. She's getting into Newport at 2.47 this afternoon. Will I be glad! I haven't had a word out of her all the time I've been here.'

She led me into the kitchen where Rosie was sitting in a rocking-chair, looking into the fire. 'It's the Vicar, Rosie,' she said. Rosie never looked up but kept staring into the flames as if mesmerized by them. I took a kitchen chair and brought it alongside her. When I caught hold of her hand, it was ice-cold. 'I'll make a cup of tea,' said Gwen, and disappeared into the scullery.

I held on to Rosie's hand, which was lifeless. Words refused to pass her lips. I looked at her face which was drained of colour and resembled a death-mask. The only sound was of Gwen taking the lid off the kettle and filling it and replacing the lid, followed by the rattle of cups in the kitchen sink. Its very ordinariness relieved the tension in me. I felt my fingers loosening the vice-like grip which I had unwittingly inflicted on Rosie's hand. Now we both stared into the fire and a strange peace came upon me. I knew that the only comfort I could give her was by sitting quietly by her side and mutely witnessing her grief. It was not something I could even begin to share but it was something for which I could show my sympathy by simply holding her hand.

I stayed there for at least an hour, never saying a word. Then, suddenly, there was the sound of the hooter from the colliery. My blood ran cold. It was the sound we had missed in the noise and excitement of our first stage rehearsal the night before – one which I had prayed earnestly not to hear again. Rose was unmoved. I left her still staring into the fire.

I went into the parlour where Gwen had closeted herself. She came to meet me as I opened the door. 'It sounds like more trouble, Vicar, doesn't it?' she said. 'As if there's not been enough.'

'All I hope is that it doesn't mean my wife has got to go underground again, Gwen. It is a selfish thing to say, I know, but she had more than she could stand last night without another dose. So if you don't mind I shall be off to the vicarage to phone up and find out what has happened. I'll be back later today, I expect.'

As I walked home there were little groups of people out on the streets anxiously wondering what had happened. Then, as I turned the corner into Vicarage Road, a woman came out of her house with a large smile on her face. 'They've got them out,' she shouted. 'I've just heard it on the wireless.' She went next door and banged on the door. By the time I had reached the vicarage gates, the whole street was ringing with excited voices, rejoicing in a great deliverance.

I strode down the drive and rushed to the phone to let Eleanor know the good news. Before I could speak, she said, 'It's all right, I know. Isn't it wonderful? I rang the colliery when I heard the hooter. My heart was in my mouth. When they told me the hooter was a celebration, not an alarm, I felt a great weight lift off my shoulders. Bed early tonight, love.'

11

'Hail, Poetry, thou heav'n born maid! Thou gildest e'en the Pirate's trade. Hail, flowing fount of sentiment. All hail! All hail! Divine Emollient.' The last time the Gilbert and Sullivan Society had given a full-throated rendering of this unaccompanied chorus from *The Pirates of Penzance* was on the last night of the performance of the opera in the Pontywen Grammar School hall. Now it was being sung with even greater fervour in the unusual setting of St Mary's Church.

Charlie Thomas loved it. 'Let's have "Hail, Poetry",' he would demand at any impromptu concert in the Lamb and Flag after rehearsal, or in the bus taking the Society for its summer outing. His untrained, rich bass voice would be unleashed with an intensity which made the other members of the bass section surplus to requirement. He would have been proud to hear how they responded to the challenge to make up for his absence.

The church was so full for the service that the attendance reached the peak of 'standing room only', something that even the Harvest Festivals throughout the years had never reached. It was a fitting testimony to a man whose sense of humour and kindliness had made him much loved by the community from which he had been snatched in a moment of time. In the front pew sat Rosie, her sister and her husband. It was the only pew with any space left. The widow sat with her head bowed throughout the service. She did not look up once. She did not shed a tear. It was as if she had died with Charlie. All that was left of him was in the coffin. All that was left of her was a living shell. She died less than a year after him, another victim of the colliery disaster.

In the meanwhile the mayor was organizing a civic service to commemorate the twelve miners who had been killed. He had not consulted me but had gone to the Reverend Elias Evans, the Minister of Tabernacle Baptist Church. 'It's the biggest place of worship in Pontywen, as it were, Vicar. There'll be far too many people wanting to come if we had it in your church. He said he would take the service, if you will say the few words, as it were, since you are my chaplain. I had suggested that you would do the prayers, as it were, but he said that if you are not accustomed to spontaneous prayer it would be better if you did something else.' He made it sound as if I were second-rate.

When I told Eleanor she said, 'After what happened at the last civic service I would have thought that the last place he would have wanted you to occupy was the pulpit. I expect he thinks that you would hardly be controversial in a memorial service, or would you, love?' She looked at me as if she were daring me to be controversial.

'Since I am more used to spontaneous sermons than to spontaneous prayer, I shouldn't like to say. It depends upon what happens between now and the service, I suppose. I can tell you one thing, my sweetheart, it will come as much from my heart as Elias Evans' prayers. I can tell you one other thing, I expect he will have as shrewd an idea of what he is going to say in his spontaneity, as I shall have in my few words off the cuff, "as it were".'

Pontywen was slowly recovering from the unwelcome prominence thrust upon it by the disaster. News reporters from the national press and even the Pathe Gazette film crew had visited the town and interviewed survivors. As the days went by and the funerals of the twelve were over, the little town settled down to semi-normality. It would be a long time, if ever, before life became the same as in the pre-disaster years.

The two-monthly Parochial Church Council meeting provided me with an opportunity to shift the focus of attention from the pit disaster to the innovation I had been considering for a while, namely, the formation of a men's club. When I suggested to the council that it should meet in a pub, there was instant opposition from Ezekiel Evans who was on his feet before I could enlarge further on what I had in mind.

'Vicar, h'I can't believe what h'I'm 'earing. Public 'ouses are for the consumption of beer, not for church meetings. Think what the Temperance Society will say, let alone the Nonconformist ministers. Their pulpits will 'ave a field day h'at the church's expense. Beer and the Bible don't mix, h'I can h'assure you.'

'Mr Evans, if you will sit down and allow me to continue, you will have a clear idea of what I am suggesting. The "Prince of Wales" has a large room at the back of the premises where the Pontywen Silver Band rehearse. There is an entrance to it from the outside. If you do not wish to visit the bar, Mr Evans, all you have to do is to stay in the room. I am sure we can come to some arrangement with the landlord whereby he can provide us with light refreshments. Those who wish to drink a pint of beer with their sandwiches may do so and those who are abstainers can have their cup of tea or a glass of lemonade. One other thing, Mr Evans, don't forget that the Deanery Chapter of Clergy always have their meeting in the back room of the "Bull" public house, Tremadoc. I feel it will be much more congenial to enjoy a drink and listen to a talk or have a discussion away from the confines of the church hall.'

'Hear, hear!' chorused a number of voices.

David Vaughan-Jenkins, the people's warden, rose to speak. 'May I congratulate you, Vicar, on a splendid idea. If we are to increase the number of men in our congregation, there is much more likelihood of that happening when we meet in what has been a social centre in the community for generations, the inn or the tavern or the pub, call it what you will. Don't forget, Mr Evans, that in the Middle Ages, many a church had its own ale house. By the way, Vicar, have you any thoughts on a name for the club? Something short and snappy, unlike a title like "The Pontywen Church Gilbert and Sullivan Society", if you will pardon the reference.'

'I take your point about our G&S group, Mr Vaughan-Jenkins, but I am afraid we are stuck with that now. As for the new club, I had thought we could connect it with the centenary and call it the Centurion Club.'

'If you don't mind my saying so, Vicar, that sounds more appropriate for a Roman Legion Club. We already have the British Legion Club in Pontywen.' The warden looked disappointed that his witticism was received with dead-pan faces.

'Before we talk about a name for a club, let's decide if we are going to have one.' Bertie Owen stood up and surveyed his audience in his best shop-steward manner. 'What's wrong with the old Church of England Men's Society that we had years ago, before Canon Llewellyn put the kybosh on it? The diocesan organization needs more recruits, so the Secretary tells me. There is strength in numbers, not in splitting up into little tin-pot groups. I demand that first of all, Vicar, you put your proposition to the vote. Let's have a democratic procedure.'

'By all means, Mr Owen,' I said. 'Canon Llewellyn closed down the branch because he felt that there was as much strength in the diocesan organization, as you call it, as there was in the cups of weak tea which were drunk at the meetings. It is pointless expecting the men of Pontywen to be attracted to the church by a handful of men sitting around in a classroom in the church hall and contemplating their navels. Would someone like to propose that we form a men's club which will meet at the Prince of Wales?'

'As people's warden,' said David Vaughan-Jenkins, 'I have great pleasure in proposing that we form a men's club and that they hold their meetings in the back room of the Prince of Wales.'

'As Vicar's warden,' said Harold Thomas, 'I second that.'

'All those in favour?' I asked. All but two hands shot up. 'All those against?' Ezekiel Evans and Bertie Owen raised their hands and looked around defiantly. They reminded me of the song I used to sing as a child in the Band of Hope. 'Dare to be a Daniel. Dare to stand alone. Dare to pass the Public House and leave the beer alone.'

'I've got a good name for the club,' said Idris the Milk, 'what about "The Saints"? Some of us are from St Padarn's, some from St Mary's and some from St Illtyd's. The one thing we've got in common is "Saint". I know that none of us are anywhere near being saints, but we all stand for the saints whose names are in our churches.'

So it was that the Saints Club was founded in Pontywen, to the great amusement of the populace, some of whom suggested that 'Sinners' would have been more appropriate. It was decided by the Parochial Church Council that the vicar would approach Mr Jim Pritchard, the landlord of the 'Prince of Wales', about the use of his back room, and that the first meeting of the club would elect officers and committee.

The next morning I made my way to the 'Prince of Wales', arriving there an hour before opening time. Mrs Pritchard opened the door to me. She was a little sparrow of a woman in her fifties, dowdily dressed for a publican's wife, with an accent familiar in the streets of Manchester rather than those of Pontywen. Ruby Pritchard had been transferred to South Wales when her husband's playing days were over. Jim Pritchard had played rugby for some of the top clubs in South Wales, until he went north and signed on for one of the leading clubs in the Rugby League circuit. A massive man, with an impressive beer belly, he had been landlord of the 'Prince of Wales' since the immediate pre-war years. Red-faced and bespectacled, he moved with a lightness of step at odds with his size. In his heyday, he must have been an awesome sight looming down on an outside half.

'This is an unexpected pleasure, Vicar,' Mrs Pritchard said. 'I don't think we have had a parson inside these doors since we came to Pontywen.' She led me into the saloon bar where Jim was checking the levels of the upturned bottles of whisky.

'Jim, it's the Vicar.' He turned around sharply to make sure that he had heard his wife correctly. 'Good God!' he exclaimed. 'I beg your pardon, Vicar. You are the last one I thought to see. Not that I am a bad lad, but the church and the pub are in two different leagues in this part of the world. It certainly wasn't like that up north. The vicar of the parish up there used to have a Harvest Thanksgiving in the public bar – but down here, it's not respectable. The pub is beyond the pale.'

'Well, as far as I am concerned, Mr Pritchard, the pub is not beyond the pale. As a matter of fact, I want the pub to be to be very much inside the pale. I wonder if we could have a chat about something I have in mind, if you are willing to co-operate.'

'Certainly, Vicar. Would you care to come upstairs to the sitting-room? Would you like a drop of something before we go up?'

'No, thank you, it is a bit early to indulge just yet. Perhaps after we have had our chat, if you don't mind.'

'Not at all,' he said. 'Only too willing to oblige a parson.'

The sitting-room was large and comfortably furnished with an expensive three-piece suite. Its windows looked out on the coal tips which adjoined the hill above Ponty-wen. On the walls were photographs of Jim in his heyday, both in Rugby Union and in Rugby League, sometimes solo and sometimes seated among his team-mates.

'I must say, Mr Pritchard, you look a tough proposition in those pictures,' I commented.

'I suppose I was in those days. Since then I have put on a lot around my middle and lost a lot of what was on my head. I doubt if I could walk around the field nowadays, let alone run around it, believe me.'

'If it came to a competition between you and me, I bet you would leave me standing. You are still light on your feet. That's something I have never been. Anyway, that's not what I have come to talk about. Last night our

Parochial Church Council decided that we want to form a men's club and that we should like to meet in your back room, if it is possible and if you are willing. We should like to have some sandwiches with our drinks, if you could provide them. We should be meeting every month on a Friday throughout the winter.'

He looked at me wide-eyed. 'All I can say, Vicar, is that I've not been so stunned since a Wigan forward laid me out for half an hour. Yes, of course. The Pontywen Band rehearse every week there on a Wednesday but apart from that, the room is very rarely used. We shall be delighted to have you if it's only to give the pub a good name. As far as the sandwiches are concerned, you let us know how many are coming a few days before and that will be fine. I'll give you a price per person later this week if you want it by then. Now then, I know we haven't been chatting very long, but what would you say to a little drop of scotch, to seal the deal?'

That little drop turned out to be half a tumblerful, sufficient to curtail my visits for the rest of the morning.

A fortnight later on a Sunday afternoon at three o'clock, the memorial service to the miners who had been killed in the colliery disaster took place at the Tabernacle Baptist Church, a large building constructed from locally quarried stone and resembling a town hall rather than a church. It was filled to capacity. When I took my seat in the deacons' sanctum at the foot of the pulpit, it was an awesome sight. The Pontywen Male Voice Choir occupied the front of the gallery, resplendent in their dark blue blazers, proud of their recent near-success in the National Eisteddfod where they had come third in the main choral event. Behind them and around them a mass of humanity was squeezed into the available pews. At ground-floor level, the local dignitaries were seated at the front. The mayor and the councillors rubbed shoulders with Sir David Jones-Williams and other former colliery owners who were joined by the steelworks masters, the industrial giants of the district. Behind them were the relatives of the dead miners. Every available space elsewhere was filled.

I sat next to the Reverend Godfrey Thomas, Minister of Moriah Congregational Church, a friend of mine since my curate days in the parish. 'Doesn't it make you feel sick', he whispered to me, 'to see these big-wigs up in the front and those who have suffered the most in mind and spirit stuck behind them?'

'I couldn't agree more,' I replied. 'It doesn't make me feel sick but it does make me feel very angry, especially when we had all that bowing and scraping from Elias Evans when the VIPs came in.'

'Talk of the devil,' said Godfrey. 'Here he comes.' The minister swept up the steps into the big pulpit to begin the service.

After a flowery tribute to the 'leaders of the community present' and a less eloquent acknowledgement of the bereaved, he announced the hymn, reading every word of the first verse which was already known by heart by every member of the congregation: 'Guide Me, O Thou Great Redeemer'. It was sung with a fervour only to be found in Wales. Then came the first prayer addressed to 'Our great compassionate God in whose hands it lies to give and to take away'. This was followed by the lesson taken from the seventh chapter of the Book of Revelation, ending with the words 'For the Lamb which is in the midst of the throne shall feed them and shall lead them unto living fountains of waters' and 'God shall wipe away all tears from their eyes'. This was read without any attempt at dramatic effect by Godfrey Thomas but with a sincerity which spoke to the hearts of those who had cried copious tears. Then the Male Voice Choir sang 'The Lord's my Shepherd' to a setting of the tune 'Crimond'. By now a wave of emotion had swept over the whole congregation.

Now came the second part of Elias Evans' 'spontaneous' prayers. Unashamedly he played upon the feelings of those who had lost their loved ones, sometimes mentioning by name one of those who had been killed, drawing loud sobs of distress from that particular family. As I listened to the cries of those whose hearts had been broken by the tragedy which had invaded that love, I felt a wave of great anger sweep over me that he should milk the occasion for his own satisfaction while those who had exploited the killed in the past sat crowned with honour in the front pew.

As the minister announced that the Vicar of Pontywen would give the address at the end of the next hymn, 'Jesu, Lover of my Soul', I knew that I should have to abandon what I had intended to say and speak my mind. When I stepped up into the pulpit, it appeared to me that I was on a stage. It was so much bigger than the enclosed space of the pulpits in St Mary's and St Padarn's. Not only that, but because it was central and not to one side, it seemed that the congregation was mine to command. Before I began to speak, I felt I had a power complex.

'And God shall wipe away all tears from their eyes,' I announced as my text. 'Many are the tears which have flowed in Pontywen, making a river of sorrow over these past weeks. Men we have known and loved have been swept away from our midst and our hearts go out to those who have lost their loved ones. Fathers, husbands, brothers have been sacrificed to King Coal. His altar has accumulated many victims over the past hundred years or so, and now in our own town it has claimed more than a fair share.

'This community owes its existence to coal. In the middle of the last century men came from the countryside in England as well as Wales in search of work. The colliery owners provided them with the terraced houses which straddle our hillsides, paid them a pittance and took their money in the truck shops. Instead of gold dust the miners found coal dust which clogged their lungs and shortened their lives. It is true that they found fellowship, fine fellowship bonded by adversity, something that no other industry has known. It is this fellowship which will enable the people of Pontywen to cope with the calamity which has hit the town.

'We meet in the presence of God whose love for us was so great that he gave His Son to die for us. He raised Him from the dead as a pledge to us that beyond this vale of tears is another life where pain and suffering are banished. Into this life our twelve brothers have been taken by the one who alone can wipe away all tears. We commend them into His hands and pray that He will grant them rest eternal. Amen.'

As I looked down from the pulpit when I had ended my 'few words' I could see that Sir David Jones-Williams' countenance was suffused with a deep purple, as if he were about to explode in a fit of apoplexy. The mayor and mayoress had their heads together, obviously bewailing their misfortune in appointing me as chaplain. When I joined Godfrey Thomas in the deacons' enclosure he whispered to me, 'You've certainly put the cat among the pigeons, boyo. Good for you, but I shouldn't turn your back in the presence of the mayor unless you've got chain-mail protection.'

I decided to stay within the safety of my confines while the Reverend Elias Evans was escorting the honoured guests out of the chapel. However, Sir David chose to break ranks and headed for me with grim intent. 'Vicar,' he spluttered, 'by what right did you use that pulpit to preach socialist claptrap instead of the word of God? If it had not been for my forefathers, those men who came to work here would have starved to death in their hovels in the countryside. I must tell you that I shall never again set foot in St Mary's Church as long as you are the vicar there.' He turned on his heel and stalked out, bumping into one of the bereaved in the process.

'What did I tell you?' said Godfrey. 'It will be the mayor's turn next. They'll be calling you "Red Fred" from now on.'

No sooner had I entered the vicarage than the telephone rang. 'You've done it again, haven't you?' shouted the mayor. 'It was a black day when I was stupid enough to ask you to be my chaplain, my one big mistake, as it were.' With that he slammed down the receiver.

Eleanor came out from the kitchen where she was preparing our tea. 'Don't tell me,' she said, 'it was His Worship Dai Spout. Well done, love.' She kissed me lightly on my cheek.

'That's not all, love,' I replied. 'Sir David Jones-Williams, Baronet, of this parish, has informed me that he will no longer set foot in St Mary's Church as long as I am vicar here. He accused me of preaching "socialist claptrap" instead of the word of God.'

'It took guts to say your piece this afternoon. What

you said was perfectly true and it came from your heart, that was plain for all to see. Don't bother about Sir David up there in his Ivory Tower. He is not exactly a great contributor to the church, anyway. As for Dai Spout and his missus, they don't come to church but wanted to exploit it for their own glory. Well, it hasn't happened. The ordinary people of Pontywen appreciated what you said. You should have heard them outside the chapel afterwards. They are the people that count, not those pompous people in the front row. Good for you, kid. Come into the kitchen with your most devoted fan and have a cup of tea. That will put the smile back on your face, "as it were".'

Some three weeks later, the Saints were holding their first meeting in the 'Prince of Wales' to elect their officers and committee for the coming year. Greatly daring, I had invited the bishop to be their first speaker. Since I had given him such short notice, I didn't expect him to come, especially since the venue was a public house. To my amazement he had said that he was free and that he would be pleased to attend the inaugural meeting.

When Ezekiel Evans and Bertie Owen learned that the bishop was to speak at the opening of the new club, they decided that they would withdraw any objections they had to its formation. In the meanwhile the churchwardens at the three churches arranged that all the men in their congregations would be circularized about the event. Since the local press had got wind of what was to happen, there was no lack of publicity. 'Vicar turns to drink' was one headline in the *Monmouthshire Post*.

The back room of the 'Prince of Wales' was a bleak rectangle, its walls painted in a drab yellow and showing signs of urgent need of redecoration. There were some thirty or so chairs arranged in rows facing a table which was covered with a dirty green cloth and behind which were three chairs. On the walls were five photographs of the Pontywen Silver Band, taken at various stages in their history of forty years. At the other end of the room was a large table, resplendent with a spotless white tablecloth and with the refreshments laid out on the brewery-stamped plates.

A quarter of an hour before the meeting was due to start there were already forty men present, most of whom were in the saloon bar ordering their drinks. I had asked Charles to stay outside in the car park to meet the bishop and bring him round to the back-door entrance. At twenty-five past seven big Jim Pritchard heaved his way through the scrum in the doorway to the bar, escorting the bishop. 'I've rescued His Holiness from the crush in there,' he said. 'It's worse than Cardiff Arms Park. I'll bring him his gin and tonic in a minute. That's on the house, Your Holiness. Could you get a few of your men to bring more chairs in, Vicar? All I hope is the refreshments will be enough to go round.'

'My apologies, my lord, I had asked Charles Wentworth-Baxter to meet you and bring you to the back entrance.' The bishop smiled at my embarrassment. 'If genius lies in the heart of delegation, Vicar, then I am afraid you will not come into that category as long as you rely on that young man. May I say how good it is to see so many men coming to the first meeting of the new organization. The church needs to find new ways to reach the men who are on its fringe and even beyond that. I think your experiment is worthy of encouragement and that is why I am here this evening. Not just for the gin and tonic,' he added.

It seemed a long time since an extremely shy bishop had interviewed me as a young ordinand and was unable to look up from a scrutiny of his desk as I sat in front of him. As someone who had been closeted in a college up until his elevation to the episcopacy, his eight years on the bishop's bench had broadened his outlook and even given him a sense of humour.

There was still no sign of Charles by the time that everybody had been seated. He had come with me in my car not long after seven o'clock and had gone out into the car park almost immediately after arriving. Some of the men said they had seen him hanging around when they came in, but the latecomers had not encountered him. I decided to begin the meeting without him.

It was a most auspicious launch for the Saints Club. There were fifty-two men present, some of whom had to be seated on two benches which had been brought in at the back. The bishop and I sat behind the table, leaving one chair empty. I had asked His Lordship to say the opening prayers, but he insisted that I should do that as the incumbent of the parish.

'Would you all stand, please, and after a moment of silence I shall say a few short prayers.' No sooner had the moment of silence begun that it was broken by a series of muffled shouts and bangings from behind the inner wall of the room. 'Will you all be seated for the time being?' I said. 'Mr Vaughan-Jenkins and Mr Harold Thomas, would you please investigate the cause of the noise?' By now the sounds were becoming frantic.

'Your missing curate, I think, Vicar, if I am not mistaken,' murmured the bishop.

He was not mistaken. Very soon the commotion ceased. A few minutes later, the two churchwardens ushered a red-faced Charles Wentworth-Baxter into the room, to suppressed laughter from the Saints. I motioned him into the empty chair. He began to explain his absence.

'You can tell me what happened later,' I hissed. 'Now, shall we stand again and compose our thoughts before our prayers?'

It must have taken me at least a minute before I could compose my own thoughts sufficiently before opening my mouth to address the Almighty. I was engaged in a hard-fought struggle to subdue my antipathy towards my assistant, a struggle I had fought frequently on other occasions.

Ten minutes later David Vaughan-Jenkins as elected chairman had taken my seat by the bishop, and Idris Shoemaker, alias Idris the Milk, was on the other chair as secretary. A committee of four had been chosen and the Saints Club had become a reality. Suggestions for talks and activities followed in abundance. The formation of a cricket team was decided as a summer venture. Outings to places of interest, especially cathedrals, as proposed by Ezekiel Evans, were envisaged. It was left to the committee to make arrangements which would turn the proposals into a coherent programme.

When the chairman called on the bishop to address the meeting it was evident that the members of the new club were becoming thirsty. 'There will be plenty of time, gentlemen, to place your orders at the bar, after we have heard what the bishop has to say to us.'

'Thank you, Mr Chairman,' said the speaker. 'I have no wish to keep you from your liquid refreshment longer than is necessary. First of all, I wish to say how encouraged I am to see so many men at this inaugural meeting. I can only hope that the numbers will not decrease but, I trust, multiply as the years go by. Secondly, I must emphasize to you that Christianity is not all beer and skittles but involves regular worship at your parish church and not just a monthly visit to the "Prince of Wales". Thirdly and lastly, you will be pleased to know, I hope you will give your vicar all the support that his leadership deserves. He is a young man with a fresh outlook on the work of a parish priest. Don't let him down. Now, if you will stand, I shall give you my blessing.'

Later, when the refreshments had been eaten, the bishop had departed and last orders were being called at the bar, I asked Charles what had happened to him. 'Well, Fred, when you asked me to go to the car park to meet the bishop, I began to develop a stomach-ache – perhaps it was the liver and onions we had before I came out. Anyway, I had to dash to the lavatory. In my hurry and not looking where I was going, I went into the ladies instead of the gents. Then, to my horror when I had finished, I found I couldn't open the door. I had banged it shut in my desperation to get in there. I shouted and shouted and banged the door.'

'So we heard, as we were about to pray,' I said.

'Sorry about that, Fred. Well, anyway, Jim Pritchard came with a ladder and got me out. He said I had jammed the lock. He told me to use the gents next time, otherwise people may get the wrong idea about me.'

12

'What are Duck Apple and Apple and Candle?' chorused the schoolgirl members of the G. & S. at the *Gondoliers* rehearsal. The 'Saints' club committee had arranged to have a Hallowe'en party when their programme was first planned. A fortnight before the event, I suggested to them that they might ask the Gilbert and Sullivan Society to join them for the occasion. This was received with enthusiasm, possibly because it meant the presence of the nubile young ladies of the chorus. When Hubert Evans, who was known to be tied to his wife's apron strings, proposed that spouses should be invited also, the proposition was turned down because there would be too many at the party.

'Duck Apple', I explained, required a large tin bath of water on which were floating a number of apples. Three competitors from either side, kneeling outside the bath with their hands behind their backs, had to catch an apple in their mouths. The first three to achieve the feat won that particular round. After the final of 'Duck Apple' came 'Apple and Candle' which involved a candle and an apple suspended on the end of two pieces of string. The participants were blindfolded and given a stipulated amount of time to catch an apple. Once again their hands had to be behind their backs, with the added disadvantage that a mouthful of wax was less agreeable than a mouthful of water.

The invitation was greeted with even greater eagerness

by the *Gondoliers* contingent, especially by the younger element, who were intrigued by the thought of the Hallowe'en games. A joint committee to organize the evening was set up, chaired by Idris the Milk since he was a member of both organizations. Another person on the committee was Bronwen Wentworth-Baxter, assistant tea lady at the G. & S. rehearsals. (Bronwen was now well advanced in her pregnancy, with the baby due in two months' time.)

Whilst she was the embodiment of serenity, Charles was the epitome of anxiety. The prospective father appeared at the daily morning service, looking more and more haggard as each day passed. 'If you don't relax,' I told him, 'your wife will be less troubled by labour pains than the phantom ones which you will experience.'

'I can't help it,' he replied. 'Bronwen is forever telling me not to be so concerned, but she's such a petite little thing, isn't she? She is not like Harold Thomas's wife for example, big and strong. Somebody was telling me the other day that she used to have babies like shelling peas – all over in an hour at most, sometimes before the midwife could get there. Bronwen is a different proposition, say what you like. I know she is in the best of hands, with Eleanor looking after her, but she means so much to me and if anything went wrong, I don't know what I would do, I can tell you.'

'Forget the "buts", Charles, and try to be positive. Eleanor says that everything seems in line for a straightforward delivery of a healthy baby. You should be encouraging your wife, not annoying her by sticking a chair behind her bottom at every hour of the day, to make her take the weight off her feet. She is not an invalid. Bronwen is simply in the process of bringing a child into the world, which is why God made her and gave her the means to do it, with your help, of course. That is why she needs your help as much *now*, as when you started the process last March. You owe that to her, believe me. Today I'll give you something to get you away from underneath her feet. You can do the communions at the hospital this morning and then visit the faithful in Sebastopol and Inkerman Street this afternoon.'

It was the day before the Hallowe'en party.

'I promised I would get the balloons for the party this morning and some other things that she wants. Then this afternoon I was going to blow up the balloons.' He looked like a child who had been deprived of a treat for a misdemeanour.

'Look, Charles, you can get those things this morning after the communion. As for you blowing up the balloons this afternoon, you can do it tomorrow. In any case, I doubt if you could achieve that feat. By the time you had blown up one of them, I wouldn't mind betting that you would have shrivelled it up seconds later, by failing to tie a knot at its top. I am sure that Bronwen will do a much better job of that than you can. You will be doing something much more worthwhile by visiting those two streets, and please don't just knock once gently at a door and then walk away quickly, writing "out" in your visiting book.'

When I returned to the Vicarage from the service, Mrs Watkins, our daily, informed me that Dewi Jones, the retired missionary from China who had taken charge of Llanhyfryd, had telephoned. "E said 'e would ring again later this morning. Dr Secombe told me to tell you that she've 'ad to go to the 'ospital after she've done 'er visits, so she won't be 'ere for lunch. She've asked me to make you some sandwiches before I go. Arthur 'ave brought in some lovely tomatoes from the green'ouse. So that should make you a nice little snack.'

I had seen very little of Dewi lately. His wife's rheumatoid arthritis had reached the stage where she had become housebound. As a result, apart from taking his Sunday services out in the country, he was not much in evidence in Pontywen. They were a delightful couple and, up until Mrs Jones's incarceration, they had been frequent visitors at the Vicarage, regaling us with tales of their time in China.

When Mrs Watkins retired to the kitchen, I went into the study to write my monthly letter for the parish magazine I had originated. Previous to its inception, the only parish news printed was in a deanery publication which came out quarterly. I had been editor of the school magazine and later in college I had been in charge of their publication. Earlier in the year, a recently 'demobbed' regular soldier had set up a small printing works in the town. It was a golden opportunity for me to realize my ambition as the editor of a monthly magazine. The Parochial Church Council had given it its blessing and the sales were sufficient to make a small profit, after I had canvassed all the shops in Pontywen for advertisements. The letter had to be done that day to meet the deadline.

Since I was writing just two days before All Saints Day, I decided I would write a job description for a saint. 'Wanted,' I began. 'A human being, not a plaster saint. Someone who knows his or her own faults and is prepared to do something about them. Must be able to laugh at himself or herself and not at other people but only with them.'

At that moment the telephone rang. I left my desk

thinking that I must arrange for the instrument to be on my desk and not on the hall table. It was Dewi Jones. 'Sorry to disturb you, Fred, but I'm afraid that I have bad news for you. I shall not be able to take the service in Llanhyfryd this Sunday. Rachel's condition has worsened and our doctor feels that perhaps a visit to the hospital in Bath for patients like herself might at least relieve the pain, if nothing else. I shall stay in Bath for the time being. If necessary I shall have to stay for a few weeks. I shall let you know about that in due time. She has told me that she does not need me with her in Bath, and that I would be doing more good in Llanhyfryd. I have told her otherwise. I'm sure you will agree, Fred.'

'Of course, Dewi. I have just began to write the "Dear Friends" letter for the magazine on the subject of Saints. I think Rachel is a prime candidate for selection in that category even though she would deny that most emphatically. Stay in Bath as long as you like. She will need you more than the congregation at St Illtyd's, much as they love you.'

'Bless you, Father. I am sure that our friend the Archdeacon will be able to supply you with a locum for the time being. Once Rachel returns, I shall be only too pleased to resume my care of the little church. I have grown to love it and the people.'

'The feeling is reciprocal, I can assure you; I hope the hospital and its waters will do her a power of good. See you when her treatment is over. Give her our love and tell her that our thoughts and prayers are with her, as always.'

I put the receiver down and then phoned the Archdeacon immediately. The Venerable Griffith Williams was an ambitious cleric, tipped by many as the next bishop of the diocese, a forecast shared by himself. As I waited for him to answer, I compared him with Rachel Jones and decided that he would be a non-runner in the saintliness stakes. The last thing he would ever do would be to laugh at himself, or if it came to that, to laugh with other people. Abraham Lincoln is reported to have said that every man over the age of forty is responsible for his face. The Archdeacon's visage wore a perpetual frown and he was fifty-three years of age.

'Archdeacon speaking,' intoned the voice at the other end. He never spoke. He always intoned.

'Fred Secombe, Vicar of Pontywen here, Mr Archdeacon. I wonder if you can help me. The Reverend Dewi Jones has been helping me at Llanhyfryd, as you know. Unfortunately his wife has to go into hospital at Bath for treatment of her rheumatoid arthritis. Dewi is going to stay nearby, to keep her company for the next few weeks at least. If you could find someone to help me, I should be more than grateful.'

'Now let me see. Would you hold on while I consult my list of retired clergy, Vicar?' There was a two-minute silence. 'Hello! Yes, I think I have someone who can help you. I am afraid he is rather old and will need to be picked up to take the services. He is the Reverend William Glossop; William Glossop who lives at number thirty-three, thirty-three Blaenavon Road, Blaenavon Road, Cwmtydfil, Cwmtydfil.' If he carries on like this, I said to myself he will earn himself the nickname of Dai Duplicate or Little Sir-Echo. 'Have you got that, Vicar?'

'I have indeed. Thank you very much, Mr Archdeacon. Is he on the phone?'

'Yes, he is. I am afraid that he is rather deaf. So you will have to speak up. The number is Cwmtydfil 979,

Cwmtydfil 979. Oh! One other thing. Because of his age he suffers from bladder bother. Perhaps you could arrange for a receptacle to be in the vestry. Occasionally he has to slip out during the singing of a hymn.'

Evidently the congregation at St Illtyd's were due for some surprises from their temporary parson, with his sudden departures to the vestry. Perhaps he would drop off to sleep like some of the ancient clergy at the Deanery Chapter meetings.

With these thoughts in mind, I rang Cwmtydfil 979. I waited for what seemed an eternity to get a reply. When I was about to put the receiver down there was a click as the ringing tone ceased. I waited another eternity before a voice quavered, 'Who is speaking, please?'

I expanded my lungs and bawled, 'This is the Vicar of Pontywen.'

'You needn't shout, Vicar. What do you want?'

'The Archdeacon says that you might be willing to take the services for the next few Sundays at Llanhyfryd Parish Church.'

'Where?'

'At Llanhyfryd Parish Church.'

'You're shouting again, Vicar. Did you say Llandovry Parish church?'

'No. Llanhyfryd Parish Church, which is linked with the parish of Pontywen.'

'Oh, you are the young man who has turned to the public house to hold his meetings there. I must tell you that as a lifetime abstainer I don't agree with that.'

'I'm sorry about that, Mr Glossop, but can you take these Sunday services for me?'

'Well, only if you send someone to pick me up. What time are your services?'

'Eleven o'clock and half past six.'

'Yes, I think I shall be able to come. Ask them to be here early and will you arrange for a chamber pot to be in the vestry?'

'Thank you, Mr Glossop. Yes, I shall see that your chauffeur will be with you in plenty of time and that some kind of receptacle will be there for your use in the vestry.'

'Very well, Vicar. Shall I be reimbursed?'

'The churchwardens will pay you two guineas a service.'

'Thank you very much. The old age pension is not much to live on these days. I'm a widower, you see. We managed when my wife was alive but I find it very difficult now I am on my own. It's a lonely life now.'

He was about to expand on the theme of loneliness when I had to apply the guillotine to any further conversation. The magazine was demanding my attention in the study, with its job description of a saint. I decided to add one further qualification to the others I had in mind – patience. I found that, as I became more involved in the various activities of a parish priest, my tolerance level was diminishing rapidly and my ministry was impaired as a result.

I finished my parish letter and added a note about Rachel Jones's visit to hospital with the subsequent arrival of the Reverend William Glossop to replace Dewi Jones for the time being at Llanhyfryd. When I had finished, Mrs Watkins tapped on the study door to let me know that she was leaving and that she had prepared some 'lovely' sandwiches for me on a plate in the kitchen. No sooner had I sat down with *The Times* crossword at my elbow and Mrs Watkins' lunchtime treat in front of me, than the telephone made its presence known yet again.

'The Vicar of Pontywen speaking,' I snarled.

'What a way to greet your loving wife, Frederick! Have you had a bad morning?'

'Sorry, love. It began with Dewi apologizing for the fact that he can't take services for the next few weeks and it ended with a request for a chamber pot from his stand-in. In between came the nasal strains of the Archdeacon intoning a series of repeats.'

'It all sounds very interesting, my dear. You must fill me in with further details later. I am afraid I have to add to your headaches by informing you that it looks as if I shall not be with you until well after our normal evening meal time. I am speaking from the hospital. The gynae-cologist is away for a few days and Matron has asked me to superintend a very tricky delivery case which could even go on until the early hours of the morning. Anyway I'll ring you again later on. I suggest you get yourself some fish and chips. That should be enough to tide you over. I tell you what, I would rather have that than hospital food any day. I'll be in touch.'

When I had finished my meal of Mrs Watkins' sand-wiches and completed *The Times* crossword by guessing the answers to two of the clues, I turned my attention to the magazine once more. After enumerating the various qualities required for the job description of saintliness, I strove to finish with a long purple passage. It shrank into a small patch of two sentences after many trials and errors. 'Only those who find that they cannot exist with-out communion with God, any more than they can exist without breathing, need apply. Only those who do not apply will be considered.' As I sat admiring my punchline it occurred to me that I had been eliminated already since pride was the deadliest of all sins. Any further contempla-tion was ended by a ring on the doorbell.

It was Idris the Milk, still wearing his apron. 'Sorry to disturb you. I've got Daisy tied up outside before I take her back to the stable. Just a quick word about tomorrow. I've just taken our tin bath down to the "Prince of Wales" on the cart, ready for the Duck Apple. Jim Pritchard is under the impression that he is supposed to be supplying the refreshments as he normally does. Bertie Owen had said that he would let him know that we were doing our own thing just for this once. Gwen and Bronwen have organized everything. Loads of people have promised sandwiches and cakes. I know I'm stupid to let Bertie be responsible for letting Jim know but he was so definite he would do it – I wonder if you could go and have a word with him. He could stop us going there, the mood he's in at the moment, if we don't pay for his food.'

'Thanks, Idris,' I replied. 'What on earth made you allow Bertie to pass on a message? He's as reliable as the Pontywen bus timetable. What do you expect me to do with Jim Pritchard? He's twice my size so I can hardly confront him.'

'I thought maybe you could use diplomacy, Vicar. You're good at that. You know, butter him up a bit. The pub closes at 3 o'clock. When I got there he was busy pulling pints. If you get him after closing time perhaps he'll be more relaxed.'

'I'm glad you said relaxed, Idris. I should think the last person he wants to see when he's putting his feet up is me.'

An hour later I was knocking on the back door of the 'Prince of Wales'. Sabre, the Alsatian guard dog, began to bark in menacing tones. 'Quiet! you stupid bloody dog.' It was difficult to know which of the two sounds was the more threatening. When the door was opened, the landlord eyed me with a mixture of surprise and suspicion. 'Good afternoon, Vicar! Come on in, will you? Do you mind sitting in the saloon bar while I check on the optics and one or two other things?'

So much for the feet-up supposition of Idris, I said to myself. As I sat on the edge of one of the red leather-topped stools I launched into the deep. 'I've just been talking to Idris the Milk, Jim, and he tells me that there has been a mix-up about the catering for tomorrow night's Hallowe'en party. Apparently Bertie Owen should have told you two weeks ago that the Saints Club were being joined for the event by the Gilbert and Sullivan Society, and the two of them would be responsible for the refreshments on that evening. Why on earth Idris relied on him to tell you, I don't know.'

'You can say that again, Vicar. Everybody knows what Bertie's like. The result is that I've ordered everything for the "do" and it's too late to stop it now. I get my stuff from the Co-op and I can't see them agreeing to cancel the food at less than a day's notice. As far as I'm concerned, they'll have to have the two lots of refreshments and that's it.'

'Is it possible for you to sell the refreshments in the saloon bar tomorrow?'

'Look here, Vicar. When the men come in here in the evening, they've had their meal. They're coming to have a drink, not a nibble on a sandwich. As you know, almost all of them are from the pit or the steelworks. If they are going to eat, it's the knife and fork for them and a hot meal, not a couple of sandwiches and cakes. I think you had better tell Idris and his committee, if they're going to come here tomorrow night, they've got to pay for the refreshments we've got for them. If they want to have the use of this room in the future, they either do that or it's back to your church hall.'

'Fair enough, Jim. I should think that by the time they have exhausted their energy in all the games they have arranged, they will be only too willing to have a double dose of sandwiches and cakes.'

By the time I had been refreshed by the use of Jim's optics, I felt fortified enough to call in at number one Hillside Avenue, the abode of Idris and Gwen, to pass on the news of my abysmal failure at the 'Prince of Wales'. Their house resembled Dr Barnardo's, in that their door was always open. 'It's me,' I called out and walked down the passage to the closed living-room door.

'Come on in, Vicar,' Gwen shouted.

When I entered the room I was greeted by the sight of a glowing fire inside the immaculately black leaded grate. Whether it was high summer or deepest winter, there was always that fire blazing away, the focal point. Beside it, Idris dozed in the afternoon when he came home from his work, and around it the family met for meals and conversation. 'We're out here,' she announced. I went into the scullery where I discovered my curate's wife with a bulging pinafore, assisting the milkman's wife. Gwen was rolling out pieces of pastry while Bronwen was using a circular cutter to make the tarts. 'The G & S incorporated!' I said.

'You could say that, but more important, how did you get on with Jim Pritchard? Idris said he had asked you to have a word with him about the refreshments. He's been worried sick since he came back from the "Prince of Wales". It's a bit much to ask people to pay for refreshments after they have given so much food themselves.'

'I'm very sorry, Gwen, but I have to admit I got

nowhere. He said that he had ordered the food from the Co-op and that they would refuse to cancel the order at the last minute. If we didn't pay for the food, there would be no more meetings in the "Prince of Wales". I can see his point of view only too clearly. I thought it was a hopeless exercise before I went there.'

'So did I, to be honest,' she replied. 'I told Idris it was a bit much asking you to go and see him anyway. Let's go into the living room and have a cup of tea. Take the weight off your feet, what do you say, Bronwen?'

Mrs Wentworth-Baxter grimaced. 'Don't say that, please. I get enough of that from my husband. If I listened to him I would have to stay in bed until the baby is born. What would happen to the house and to our meals, I dread to think.'

No sooner had we sat down than Idris appeared. 'Well?' he inquired when he saw me.

'What did you expect? It's pay up or get out. I can't say I blame him. You know where the blame lies.'

The people's churchwarden collapsed into his armchair at the fireside. 'I'll never rely on Bertie Owen ever again.'

'How many times have you said that before?' said Gwen. 'You know what he's like. Let's get the kettle on the fire and have a cuppa. I hope you've learnt your lesson. Do it yourself next time, not leave it to Bertie.'

Half an hour later, Idris was fast asleep, mesmerized by the coal fire. 'I think I had better be off.' I whispered.

'He's so rude, isn't he?' said his wife, also in a whisper. 'I think Bronwen and I had better finish our work.'

Some two hours later I was taking my place in the queue for the fish and chips at Cascarini's Fish Bar in Pontywen Square. There was the usual motley throng of housewives, husbands who had been sent out to get 'two cutlets and six penn'orth' while the table was being laid, and children who brought the order written on a scrap of paper, wrapped around the coins necessary for payment. One of these children was Tommy Harris, the scourge of St Padarn's Sunday school. As I joined the queue he was in the middle of an altercation with another boy in front of him. 'Stop pushing me,' said Tommy's opponent.

'I wasn't pushing you,' came the reply.

'He was, wasn't he, mister?' appealed the boy to a steelworker standing behind Tommy. The man was still wearing the sweat rag around his neck, fresh from his labours at the furnace. 'Don't ask 'im. 'Ow could 'e tell?' said Tommy.

'You keep your mouth shut, young 'Arris. I could see you was pushing 'im.'

'If it comes to that, you was pushing me behind me.'

'Any more lip from you, Tommy, and I'll give you a clip around the ear.'

'You and who else?'

As the steel-worker was about to administer the punishment, 'young 'Arris' noticed me standing behind him. ''Allo, Vicar,' he said brightly and then turned to face the front of the queue. 'Sorry, Vicar,' said the man, 'but 'e's asking for it. Always causing trouble, or spoiling for a fight.'

'You needn't tell me that,' I replied. 'I know him quite well. He comes to our Sunday school at St Padarn's.'

'I know 'im quite well too. 'E lives next door but one to me, a proper little bugger, I can tell you. Perhaps you can teach 'im some manners at your Sunday school. 'Is parents 'aven't been able to do it, that's positive.'

By now the little fracas had become the centre of

attention amongst the customers; Giuseppe Cascarini, whose accent was redolent of the valleys rather than of Naples, his place of origin, was more interested in what was happening in his shop than he was in the state of the chips in the pan. I felt I had to jump to Tommy's defence. 'Well, Mr, er . . . Lewis,' I said. 'Well, Mr Lewis, we are not all saints by any means. I am certainly not one. He's not a bad lad. Tommy has plenty of guts and a keen sense of humour. What's more, he's a very good brother to the two children in his family, so I should remember that, if I were you.'

He glared at me, swallowed hard and kept silence for the rest of the time he was in the shop.

When it came to my turn at the counter I thought I had better order two fish and chips, in case Eleanor came home earlier than expected. 'I must apologize, Vicar, for the bit of a row earlier on,' said Giuseppe. 'You know what it is like when they send the kids. But there you are, one and ten pence, please.'

As I came out from the shop, I was met by Tommy. 'Thank you, Vicar,' he said. 'I didn't 'ear properly what you said, but it shut old 'Arry up, that's more than his missus does, that's for sure.'

'You must learn not to be so cheeky, then you won't get into trouble. You had better run home with those fish and chips otherwise your parents will want to know why they're cold.'

It was a chilly, starry night with a hint that November would bring some early snow to the valleys, when the calendar changed in a day's time. I shivered in the biting north-east wind. The kitchen was warm and welcoming when I came in through the back door. I opened the oven and put the parcel of Cascarini's best, wrapped in the

Daily Herald, on the top shelf. Leaving my overcoat on, I filled the kettle, ready for a pot of tea to supplement my meal. No sooner had I turned the tap off than there was a ring on the telephone.

'Get that kettle on,' came the voice at the other end. 'I'll be with you in a quarter of an hour or so.'

'There's more than a cup of tea waiting for you. How do you fancy a cutlet of hake and six penn'orth of chips, fresh from Cascarini's.'

'Wonderful,' said my wife. 'And I wouldn't object to a tot of whisky to start with; I need it, believe me.'

'You don't sound very happy, love.'

'I'll tell you all about it when I get back and that can't be too soon.'

By the time she came home I had laid the table in the dining-room instead the kitchen. The bunch of chrysanthemums from our garden, picked that afternoon by Arthur, our part-time gardener, now joined the condiments instead of reposing on the window ledge of the sitting-room. With all the bars on the electric fire on full blast, the temperature had moved from the igloo stage to the almost bearable when I heard the car coming down the Vicarage drive. As she opened the door I met her with a half a tumblerful of whisky in my hand. 'How about that for service, love?' I said.

She put her arms round my neck and burst into tears. I led her into the dining room and thrust the whisky into her hand. 'Drink a mouthful of this, there's a dear. Now sit down and let me cuddle you for a minute.' We sat there for quite a while with her head on my shoulder. When her sobbing had subsided she raised her head. 'That poor woman! She went through all that suffering for nothing. It was a dreadful haemorrhage, and the baby was asphyxiated. It was awful. It was a beautiful baby, a little girl. That's the first baby that I have lost. I hope to God it's the last.' She began to weep again. Suddenly she stood up. 'I must pull myself together. This is very unprofessional. What is it that President Truman said? "If you can't stand the heat, get out of the kitchen." There's a lot of truth in that, isn't there?'

'Agreed, my love,' I said. 'Well, you are not in the kitchen, you're in the dining-room. So transfer your bottom to the dining chair and you will be served with fish and chips à la Cascarini. Finish off that whisky while the waiter disappears to bring you your main dish, hot from the oven, having been sheltered in the *Daily Herald*. I am afraid they had run out of the *Daily Worker*, otherwise it would have been well and truly red-hot.'

'Fred, that's pathetic. I know you're trying to cheer me up, but that's not worth even one gold star for trying.'

'Excuse me, teacher. I think I deserve five gold stars. You sound as if you are back to normal already. So could you please park yourself while I take charge of the kitchen?'

Later, as we drank our cups of tea, Eleanor began to put the afternoon's tragedy into perspective. 'I suppose I must have delivered dozens of babies safely since I've been in practice. There are countless more children I shall be bringing into the world in the years that lie ahead. I know that is no consolation to the mother who lost her baby today. The only consolation I have is that I could have done nothing to prevent it happening. Perhaps in the not too distant future, technology will develop to such an extent that it will be possible to make the death of a baby at childbirth a rarity.'

'Well, very soon, my sweet, you will be bringing the first of the Wentworth-Baxter brood into this world. The sooner the better, as far as the prospective father is concerned.'

'Thank God, there should be no complications with that delivery. The baby is well placed in the womb and Bronwen is in excellent health. So all should be well.'

'There is only one caveat to that. Have you ever known a Wentworth-Baxter enterprise to be quite straightforward?'

'Secombe, that's a very wicked remark. I can only hope that you won't have to regret making it.'

13

Next morning I had a phone call from the Rural Dean. 'I wonder if I could come and borrow some Ancient and Modern hymn books from you, Vicar? We have a confirmation service here this evening. There are four other parishes bringing candidates. There are even two candidates from Trehafod. I am coming down to Pontywen to pick up some bottles of pickles we have been promised from Howells the greengrocer. Is eleven o'clock all right for you?'

'Fine by me, Mr Rural Dean. I'll have them here at the Vicarage ready for you. Are you all right for veils?'

'They are bringing their own veils with them for the female candidates. We have a few to spare anyway.'

The mention of Trehafod, a parish of one hundred and fifty souls, hidden away in the hills, reminded me of a well-known anecdote about William Rees, its incumbent for forty-six years who had died recently. It was said that at one time there had been no confirmation candidates for more than twenty years. When the Bishop inquired of the Vicar the reason for this dearth the old man replied, 'Well, my Lord, we are so much out of the way up here that it would be a long old journey for you. So I have been doing the few that we have had myself to save you the trouble.'

I was thinking about this legendary story as I went across to the church for Matins. Charles met me as I was coming up the path. 'You are early this morning,' I said.

'Can't sleep,' he replied. 'These are worrying times. It won't be long now before Bronwen's due to have the baby, as you know. I keep waking up every five minutes.'

'For heaven's sake, Charles. Eleanor has told you that you have nothing to worry about. Everything is straightforward, apparently.'

'That's not my only headache, Fred. There's the financial aspect. It's all right for you. You are well away, as an incumbent with a wife who is a doctor. Now that Bronwen has given up work, we have to rely on my curate's stipend and you know how inadequate that is.'

'In that case you will have to look for a living. Trehafod is vacant now that old William Rees has tottered into the arms of his maker. It is the kind of parish that would suit you nicely, the minimum of work, delightful countryside. You could stay there for the next fifty years or so; another William Rees. The parish is in the gift of the Bishop. I shouldn't think there would be a rush of candidates.'

'Many thanks for that vote of confidence. All the same, I think I should write to his lordship today. The sooner I get a living the better, even if it is in the middle of nowhere. It can easily be a stepping-stone to something better when the time is ripe, can't it?'

'I suppose it all depends on what you decide is the ripe time, Charles. Some times take longer than others to ripen and in your case the ripening process could be a protracted one. Anyway, let's go into the church and say our prayers about it.'

As we came into the vestry after service, he said to me, 'I have made up my mind. When I read that verse from the seventh chapter of the Wisdom of Solomon, "God loveth none but him that dwelleth with wisdom", I felt I was being guided to make a wise choice. I shall definitely write to the Bishop today.'

'Better still, Charles,' I suggested, 'why don't you come to the Vicarage now and phone him? There is no time like the present for the man of wisdom and it will save you the money you would spend in a call-box.'

'I don't know about that. Do you think he would mind a curate phoning him without giving him notice? It's a bit of a cheek, don't you think?'

'Not at all. You don't have to give written notice to the Bishop if you want to phone him. If he's busy, he will ask you to call him later. I am sure that he will not regard you as impertinent. Would you like me to make the initial call and say that you wish to speak to him?'

'Thanks, Fred, that would be a great help.'

Ten minutes later, after I had made us both a cup of coffee, we went into the hall from the study, and he stood by my side, his body trembling as I dialled the Bishop's number. His secretary answered and asked me to hold on for a moment.

'What's happening?' inquired Charles.

'That was his secretary. She has asked me to hold on. He has either paid a visit to the lavatory or perhaps he hasn't quite finished his breakfast,' I whispered. Charles began to giggle nervously.

His giggle was cut short when the Bishop's voice was heard loud and clear on the receiver, which I was holding at arm's length. 'This is Fred Secombe, my Lord.'

'Good morning, Vicar. What can I do for you?' He sounded unusually abrupt.

'It's nothing you can do for me. I have Charles Wentworth-Baxter with me who wishes to speak to you. I suggested that he made the call from the Vicarage rather than a public telephone-box. I shall leave him with you, my Lord.'

I handed the receiver to my curate and disappeared into the kitchen where I had heard Mrs Watkins arriving, ready for her morning round of domestic chores. She was rubbing her hands together vigorously. 'There've been quite a few flakes of snow when I was coming down just now,' she said. She lived up on the hillside, in a row of small cottages exposed to the easterly winds.

'There's still some hot water in the kettle, if you'd like a cup of tea. It won't take long to boil up again,' I said.

'Thank you, Vicar, I'd love one if it's only to keep the cold out and that. I can drink tea until the cows come 'ome, I can.'

She sat down at the table, still clad in her coat, and launched into a recital of how many times a day she stopped for a cup of tea. Before she could reveal her evening drinking habits, there was a loud tap on the door. 'Come on in, Charles, and tell us the news.'

My curate's face spoke volumes before he uttered a word. It was split from ear to ear. 'What do you think?' he asked.

'I know. He has told you to pack in the ministry and apply for a job where perhaps you can be useful, if possible.'

'Don't be horrible, Fred. He has offered me the living of Trehafod. He said that I will not be able to move in until well into next year, because of the state of the house after old William Rees had lived there for forty-six years.'

'Congratulations, Charles. You had better get back to Bronwen as quickly as possible to pass on the good news. I expect she will be glad to know your offspring will be breathing the pure air of Trehafod instead of the polluted variety we have to endure in Pontywen. She will be nearer to her mother up there, too.'

'Why did you have to mention that? That is something I hadn't thought of. That is a decided disadvantage. I bet Bronwen thinks so, too. Still, we may not be there very long, you never know. The great thing is I can be my own boss once I am there.'

'Thank you, Charles. You make me sound like an ogre instead of your best friend.'

'You know what I mean. Of course you are my best friend and you have been very good to me, much more than I have deserved, I must admit. The thing is, I have reached a watershed in my life. I am about to become a father. I need now to stand on my own two feet.'

'Well, use those two feet to get home *tout de suite* before the hot news begins to cool. Mrs Watkins says it is beginning to snow.'

Promptly at eleven o'clock the Rural Dean was on my doorstep with an empty carrier bag in his hand. 'Twenty hymn books will be sufficient, Vicar. We've got sixty in the church. If this snow begins to fall properly, we'll be lucky to have eighty for the service. I won't stay, if you don't mind. Too much to do, you see.' As he was putting the books into his carrier bag, I told him that Charles had been offered the living of Trehafod. 'Very good,' he said. 'It will be a change for them to have a young man. It will be nice to have another young vicar at the Chapter meetings too. In any case, old William Rees never came to one for the forty-six years he was in the parish. No wonder the Archdeacon called him Robinson Crusoe.' He began to laugh at this witticism. He was still laughing as he got into his car. 'Robinson Crusoe! Ha! ha!'

Eleanor was not laughing when she came home after

morning surgery and her post-surgery visits. There was a thin layer of snow on the roof and the bonnet of the car. 'The top of the valley is like the Arctic,' she said. 'It won't be long before the snow settles on the roads. Thank heavens I have finished my visits for today.' She sniffed the aroma which was coming from the kitchen. 'And thank heavens Mrs Watkins is the chef for today.' We had decided to have a midday meal because of the Hallowe'en feast at the 'Prince of Wales'.

As we sat down to our bowls of 'cawl', mutton soup with a wide range of vegetables, I told her about the Wentworth-Baxter promotion. 'Well, he has made it, after all,' she commented. 'I never thought he would. All I can say is that he owes it to you. No other vicar would have had your patience to suffer him for so long, believe me.'

'In fairness to him, love, he did admit that I had been very good to him, much more than he had deserved.'

'You can say that again. I am so glad for Bronwen's sake. If they had to try to cope with the baby, on a curate's stipend, it is she who would have suffered. I expect the Bishop felt that the parish of Trehafod was the one place in the diocese where he could do the least harm. That makes two of your curates in splendid isolation, both of whom, I am willing to bet, will remain there indefinitely.' The other curate to whom Eleanor referred, was the Reverend Barnabas Webster, a somewhat elderly late entrant into holy orders who had left his village shop to serve the Lord instead of his customers. I soon discovered that he would have been better employed serving his customers. In an exercise of damage limitation, the Bishop had exiled him to a sparsely populated rural parish where he was happy being his own boss, as Charles wished to be.

'Perhaps now, Frederick, the Bishop will find you an assistant curate who will assist rather than hinder.'

'I don't know about that, love. Curates are not in plentiful supply nowadays. Once the post-war input of candidates gets out of the colleges and into the parishes, things will be different. Another couple of years should see that happening.'

'For your sake, my dear, I hope it is sooner than that. With three churches to look after and just one geriatric with bladder bother to help you, you will be hard put to advance the frontiers of the Kingdom of God in Pontywen.'

Later that afternoon I went down to the garden shed to sort out some apples for the Hallowe'en games. There were now only a few snowflakes in the air and it looked as if the weather would be no hindrance to the success of the evening. Eleanor was busy baking some Welsh cakes on the stove top when I came back into the kitchen with a basketful of apples. 'All is safely gathered in,' I sang, ''ere the winter storms begin.'

'You're a bit late there, Fred. There are still three trees to be plundered and the snow has arrived already. It's probably a memo from the Almighty, that it's time you finished your apple harvest. Arthur asked you weeks ago, whether you wanted him to pick them, but, no, you said, you wanted to do that job. The poor man thinks you don't trust him.'

'He knows perfectly well that I trust him. You can ask him that yourself, if you don't believe me. He'll be there tonight.' Arthur Williamson, retired delivery man for the Co-op Bakery, had been my part-time gardener for the past twelve months, and had transformed the kitchen garden.

'I'm just pulling your leg, Secombe. I know that the only motive you have for picking the apples yourself is pride of possession. All this fruit is mine. I would not want to upset Arthur's evening anyway.'

By the time we arrived at the 'Prince of Wales' the back room was full of excited noise and activity. The female chorus of the Gilbert and Sullivan Society were chasing each other around the bath of water, which occupied the centre of the floor space. All the chairs were lined up against the walls, many of them occupied by the 'saints' with their beer glasses in their hands, enjoying the spectacle of the young maidens besporting themselves. The landlord had brought in the piano from the public bar and placed it next to the table, on which was laid out an impressive array of refreshments. When we came in Charles and Bronwen came to greet us. It must have been the first occasion at a function that Charles had been present before I had arrived. The couple were in such a state of exhilaration that it was obvious to all that their cup was brimming over. To my amazement Bronwen came up to me and kissed me. 'Thank you for getting the Bishop to give Charles his new job. It's going to mean so much to me.' Then she turned to Eleanor and hugged her.

'Be careful with that lump, young lady,' warned my wife. 'It hasn't got that much longer to stay there but I know how you must feel. I'm so glad for you, Bronwen.' Charles stood by, saying nothing but grinning like a Cheshire cat, enjoying the prospect of becoming both father and vicar.

Idris the Milk had been appointed by the joint committee as MC for the evening. 'Will you all fill up your glasses in the next quarter of an hour?' he bellowed. 'After that no one is allowed to sneak out to the bar until the interval. We have got a full programme of games and music. So hurry up and get your liquor or your lemonade. Don't forget, girls. No booze for you: stay in here and don't go into the bar, Gwen will take all your orders in here.'

They crowded around his wife shouting their orders. 'Hold on, girls. Give me a chance,' she pleaded. 'Wait your turn and I'll write down what you want.' She produced a writing pad from her handbag and began to write down their requirements. 'Pay me when you get your drinks. Don't bother me with money at the moment. I want two gentlemen at least to come with me to the bar to carry the trays.' There was a rush of volunteers sufficient to carry enough drinks to slake the thirst of five times the number of girls present. The young ladies had never had such a lot of attention paid them.

'Now settle down, everybody,' shouted Idris, when the procession from the bar had ended. 'Unlike most programmes, we are going to have our piece of resistance first. Vicar, will you float your delicious apples on the water in the bath, please? All these lovely apples have their stems still intact. You can either try to pick them up by the stem, or else if you have a mouth big enough, no names, no pack drill, you can try to turn the apple into a gob-stopper. Whatever happens, you must have your hands behind your back. Anybody trying to use their hands will be disqualified straight away. Now, will the first team from each side step forward and kneel by the bath. G. & S. on my right, "Saints" on my left.'

Inevitably, Bertie Owen had managed to get into the first round, representing the 'Saints', together with Arthur the Co-op, and Harold Thomas. Opposite them were three enthusiastic schoolgirls, Rachel Owen, Sally Jones and Brenda Llewellyn. Rachel was a well-built teenager.

Sally and Brenda were slim and petite. 'Now then, girls, stay where you are and Gwen will put a towel around your necks. We don't want your mothers complaining that you have been drenched. Gentlemen, you can fend for yourselves. When I blow the whistle the battle begins. Get your mouths in shape, everybody. Have you finished, Gwen? Right, off we go.' There was a loud blast on the whistle, and the attack began on the six apples floating in the water.

The first into the fray was Rachel, lunging towards the nearest apple, which had attracted the attention of Arthur as well. Their heads met across the bath with a resounding crack. It was fortunate for Arthur, with his bald head, that Rachel was as well endowed with hair as with the rest of her anatomy. In the meanwhile Bertie Owen, ignoring the MC's remark about big mouths, was attempting to capture the whole of an apple in his wide-open mouth. As he thrust his face towards an apple for the fourth time, giving the impression of a man eating shark, the top part of his set of false teeth fell into the water, to the great hilarity of spectators and competitors alike. Immediately Bertie divested himself of his jacket and began to roll up his shirt-sleeves to recover his missing denture. 'Foul!' bawled Idris. 'Off you go.'

'I'm not leaving here without my teeth,' lisped Bertie, 'foul or no foul.' He plunged his hand into the bath, splashing water over his two fellow competitors, who were unprotected from the deluge.

'We didn't ask for a baptism,' Arthur complained.

'Got em,' shouted Bertie and held aloft the dental plate, as if it were some kind of trophy. The next second, it was back in his mouth.

'That's the cleanest his teeth have been for months,'

commented Llew Jones. Eventually the contest ended with a score of nine apples to the Gilbert and Sullivan Society against three for the 'Saints'. When the game was over there was more water on the floor of the 'Prince of Wales' than there was in the bath.

'And now for a surprise item,' announced Idris. 'A duet between Mabel and Frederick, in other words, the Vicar and Mrs Vicar accompanied by our popular Curate. What you might call a clerical gathering at the piano.' It was indeed a great surprise to Eleanor, and myself, since it was some eighteen months since we had last sung that set piece from *The Pirates of Penzance*. Charles advanced towards us with a score of the operetta.

'It's all right, Charles,' I said. 'We don't need it.'

'Big head!' whispered my wife. 'For that I hope you remember your words as well as the music.'

As the opening notes sounded tinnily from the public bar instrument, the months slipped away and we were once again on stage, at the last night of the performance in the School Hall, the night we became engaged. The libretto called upon us to declare our love for each other 'till we are wed and ever after'.

'Apart from a few hesitances, Frederick, you were word perfect; I must admit I was more hesitant than you,' said Eleanor.

'It never showed,' I replied.

'Always the gentleman,' she murmured.

'The next item is in memory of our dear friend, Charlie Thomas, to be conducted by our splendid conductor, Aneurin Williams. "Hail Poetry" sung by the full chorus,' announced Idris.

'Hang on, Idris. How can we be full? We haven't had our refreshments yet.' This second interruption from

Llew Jones was greeted with groans for its lack of taste, as a prelude to a tribute to a much-loved man. 'We'll ignore that,' said the MC. 'Mr Williams, will you please take over?' Aneurin stepped forward and stood by the piano. 'Do you want a note?' he asked.

'No,' came the reply. He raised his right hand and, as he brought it down, there came a volume of sound, which shook the walls of the back room, as loud as anything produced by the Pontywen Silver Band at their rehearsals. It was one of the most moving experiences of my life. There was a long silence after the music died away; an unspoken prayer for the soul of a dear friend.

When the chorus had returned to their seats, Idris came into the centre of the room. 'There will now be a short interval for refreshments. You can have your grub now, Llew and I hope you enjoy it.' It must have been the least enjoyable meal he had ever eaten. For the next half hour, chaos reigned as the men fought their way into the bar and the volunteer waiters fought their way out of it, with trays laden with soft drinks for the girls. To add to the chaos was the scramble around the refreshment table, where Gwen and Bronwen, plus their helpers, endeavoured to cope with the inroads upon the plentiful supply of sandwiches, pickles and cakes.

Eventually, when calm had been restored, stomachs filled, and thirsts satisfied, Idris introduced the second half of the evening's entertainment. 'The piece of resistance in this second half is once again the first item, "Apple and Candle". At least in this game you won't get wet. Bertie may find his false set stuck in a candle, but at least he won't drown his pals. Gwen and Bronwen will blindfold the competitors who will come forward, one at a time. You will be given one minute to catch an apple.

Once again, it is hands behind your back. This time, one bite out of an apple will earn one point. Nobody has a mouth big enough to get it round an apple as Bertie showed us earlier on, so as soon as you have bitten one piece, not scratched the apple or left a tooth mark on it, but bitten a piece out of it, that gets you a point. If you can get two or more pieces out within two minutes it means extra points.'

The apple and the candle were suspended from an old gas bracket, at the side of the room, the chairs having been cleared away from under it. Once again, Rachel Owen was sent in to bat first for the G. and S. but, whereas she had found it easy to pick up the apple by its stem in the bath of water, she found herself biting pieces of wax rather than apple. On the other hand, the men found it easier to get at the apple by reason of their superior height. The last 'man' in for the G. & S., with two points to win, was Gwen. She had played the game many times before and knew the secret. Not for her the headlong lunge but instead the gentle stroke of her nose against the dangling object, followed by a quick bite when the apple was identified. Her three bites gave her side a clear victory, cheered loudly by the girls who were jumping up and down.

There followed various musical items. Then came the last event of the evening. 'I want all the chorus placed in the middle of the room.' said Idris, 'ready for an old favourite, musical chairs. Our excellent pianist will provide the music. Will you all give him a hand for his efforts throughout the evening?' Charles stood up at the piano and bowed as he received his ovation.

'Now, I want everybody to join in this, no sitting out. All take your place round the chairs, please.' The pianist began to play the Policeman's chorus from *The Pirates of Penzance* as Bronwen decided to join in the fun, despite the handicap of her bulge. After five rounds, when there were only ten competitors left, she was still there, unseen by her husband who had his back to the proceedings. When the music restarted, he speeded up the tempo and then stopped suddenly. Bronwen, who had been behind Arthur, whose little bandy legs had been working overtime, came into a violent collision with my part-time gardener and fell to the floor. There was a breathless hush. Charles turned round to see what was happening, to discover his wife lying on the floor. Before he could reach her, Eleanor had moved to her side. 'I feel terrible,' breathed Bronwen. 'I think something is happening.'

'Phone for an ambulance, Idris.' my wife said, in her best professional manner. 'Now then, let's get you into Jim's sitting room while we wait for the ambulance to come.'

'What on earth made you join in the game?' demanded Charles whose face was paler than that of his wife.

'Shut up, Charles,' ordered my wife, 'and help me to get her out of here.'

I followed the three of them upstairs to the sitting room where Ruby Pritchard was waiting to receive us, having been warned by her husband about what had happened.

'Would you mind if she rested on your bed while I examine her?' asked Eleanor.

'Of course not,' said the landlord's wife. 'Is there anything you want?'

'Some warm water and towels for a start.'

'Is she going to be all right?' inquired Charles, who was shaking in his anxiety.

'Of course she is,' said Eleanor. 'Now be a good boy

and go downstairs out of the way until the ambulance arrives. Get Jim to give you a good dose of whisky. That's all the medicine you need. Fred, ask Idris if he will get the party to break up, and let them know that everything is OK and that nothing terrible has happened. It is all under control.'

Charles went to the bar counter, where Jim Pritchard had prepared a large whisky for him. 'Sit over there, Reverend, in the corner. It's already past closing time so you'll have a bit of peace down here. Come on, gentlemen, drink up and get a move on, please.' The few customers who were left swallowed their beer and made a quick exit. When I went into the back room, only Idris and Gwen were left.

'Is there anything I can do?' asked Gwen.

'No, thank you,' I replied. 'Mrs Pritchard is helping Eleanor and apparently all is well.'

'The ambulance people said they would be here as soon as possible, whenever that is,' said Idris.

'Apart from the, er, incident in the last half hour, it has been a very enjoyable evening, thanks to you and, of course, Gwen, who must have worked very hard. Perhaps by tomorrow morning we shall have some good news for the parish. That will round off the enjoyment nicely.'

'I hope so, Vicar. I don't think I'll be able to sleep tonight, worrying about what has happened. Bronwen has been so happy about the baby coming.'

'I tell you what, Gwen. I'll let you know first thing tomorrow if the baby has arrived and everything is OK.' If they had waited longer they would have had the good news before they left.

When I went into the bar, Charles was taking his

second dose of medicine. 'Would you care to join your curate in a glass of whisky, Vicar?'

'With the greatest of pleasure, Jim, and many thanks.'

'I remember when our first was born up North,' said the landlord. 'The only thing that kept me going while I was waiting for the missus to deliver the goods, like, was the old whisky bottle, good old Doctor Barleycorn.'

As I glanced across at Charles, it was evident that the good old doctor was about to send him into sweet oblivion. His eyelids were almost closed.

The next second his eyes were wide open. There was a cry of a baby upstairs. 'Good God, that was quick!' exclaimed the landlord.

Charles was up on his feet instantly. 'Do you mind if I go upstairs?' he asked excitedly.

'Of course not,' replied Jim.

'Hold on, Charles, I'd better come with you,' I said. 'You can't just dash into the bedroom.'

He went up the stairs two at a time. Mrs Pritchard met us on the landing. 'I were just coming to fetch you, Reverend. You've got a little boy.' Charles began to weep.

'For heaven's sake, Charles, you can't go in to see Bronwen like that. It's time for joy that a man has been born into the world and he's your son.'

'Don't come in just yet, Charles,' shouted Eleanor. 'Everything's wonderful and you have a lovely baby boy.'

It was another quarter of an hour before the ambulance arrived. By then Bronwen was sitting up, in a nightdress borrowed from Ruby Pritchard and holding her son in her arms, watched by a husband who was still in a daze. The ambulance men put a blanket round her shoulders and led her out into the night, accompanied by Charles.

'That was one of the easiest births I have ever witnessed,' said Eleanor as we made our way home in the car. 'And what a place for a son of a parson to come into this life!'

'What do you mean, love? He was born in an inn.'

'True enough, but it was certainly more comfortable than a stable. When our first is born, I shall make sure that he or she is born in a hospital ward.'

'And when will that be, pray?' I asked.

'After tonight, I feel quite broody. In a year's time, shall we say, if not sooner.'

'Sooner, I should say,' I replied. She stopped the car and kissed me.